The Midnight Twins

JACQUELYN MITCHARD

razOr
bill

Midnight Twins

RAZORBILL
Published by the Penguin Group
Penguin Young Readers Group
345 Hudson Street, New York, New York 10014, U.S.A.
Penguin Group (USA) Inc., 375 Hudson Street, New York, New York 10014, U.S.A.
Penguin Group (Canada), 90 Eglinton Avenue East, Suite 700, Toronto, Ontario, Canada M4P 2Y3
(a division of Pearson Penguin Canada Inc.)
Penguin Books Ltd, 80 Strand, London WC2R 0RL, England
Penguin Ireland, 25 St Stephen's Green, Dublin 2, Ireland (a division of Penguin Books Ltd)
Penguin Group (Australia), 250 Camberwell Road, Camberwell, Victoria 3124, Australia
(a division of Pearson Australia Group Pty Ltd)
Penguin Books India Pvt Ltd, 11 Community Centre, Panchsheel Park, New Delhi – 110 017, India
Penguin Group (NZ), 67 Apollo Drive, Rosedale, North Shore 0632, New Zealand
(a division of Pearson New Zealand Ltd.)

Penguin Books (South Africa) (Pty) Ltd, 24 Sturdee Avenue, Rosebank, Johannesburg 2196, South Africa

Penguin Books Ltd, Registered Offices: 80 Strand, London WC2R 0RL, England

10 9 8 7 6 5 4 3 2 1

LIBRARY OF CONGRESS HAS CATALOGED THE HARDCOVER EDITION AS FOLLOWS:

MITCHARD, JACQUELYN.
  THE MIDNIGHT TWINS / BY JACQUELYN MITCHARD.
    P. CM.
  SUMMARY: IDENTICAL TWINS MEREDITH AND MALLORY BRYNN HAVE ALWAYS SHARED ONE ANOTHER'S THOUGHTS, EVEN AS THEY DREAM, BUT THEIR CONNECTION DIMINISHES AS THEY APPROACH THEIR THIRTEENTH BIRTHDAY, AND ONE BEGINS TO SEE THE FUTURE, THE OTHER THE PAST, LEADING THEM TO DISCOVER THAT A HIGH SCHOOL STUDENT THEY KNOW IS DOING HORRIBLE THINGS THAT PLACE THE TWINS, AND OTHERS, IN GRAVE DANGER.
  ISBN 978-1-59514-160-6
  [1. TWINS--FICTION. 2. SISTERS--FICTION. 3. TELEPATHY--FICTION. 4. CLAIRVOYANCE--FICTION. 5. PSYCHOPATHS--FICTION. 6. SCHOOLS--FICTION. 7. FAMILY LIFE--NEW YORK (STATE)--FICTION. 8. NEW YORK (STATE)--FICTION.] I. TITLE.
  PZ7.M6848MID 2008
  [FIC]--DC22
                                                                2007031139
Razorbill paperback ISBN: 978-1-59514-226-9

Printed in the United States of America

For Kathy and Karen, and the single sentence that inspired this book,
and for their big sister, Deb.
Everything you say is funny or beautiful.

LOOK BOTH WAYS

LOOK BOTH WAYS

M eredith and Mallory Brynn looked exactly the same.
So it was natural for people to expect them to be the same.

Of course, not all people who look the same really are.

Meredith and Mallory were identical twins. But they were opposites.

One person made into two by luck or by fate, until they were almost teenagers, they never, not once, thought of themselves as being two separate people. Identical twins often don't. They knew each other as they would never know anyone else, before they understood even the fact that they were people, before they could talk, before they had names. Yet they acted differently from each other, spoke differently, thought differently, and wanted different things. They played with different toys, laughed at different jokes, excelled at different subjects in school. Their mother stopped dressing them alike when they were just two years old, because Mallory didn't like dresses and pulled off all the buttons.

In their lives, being identical would be the easy part. Being different would bring them power, and power almost always comes paired with grief.

Most children love hearing the story of their birth, but the Brynn girls heard theirs so often that they got sick of it, even though it was, they had to admit, a pretty unusual story. Their mother, Campbell Brynn, a surgical nurse, went into labor at a New Year's Eve party. She wasn't due to have the babies for another three weeks. There was a mad dash to the hospital, where the girls' father, Tim, and Bonnie Jellico, another nurse and Campbell's best friend, held her hands while the babies came—with startling speed, quicker than anyone would have imagined for firstborn children. The doctor arrived with just moments to spare.

Meredith was older, born first at 11:59 p.m. Mallory came just two minutes later, at 12:01 a.m., the first baby of the New Year in the small town of Ridgeline, New York. With all the hands and machines and towels and instruments freewheeling around the delivery room (because when twins are born, there needs to be two of everything—two newborn specialists, two neonatal nurses, two warming beds), it took a while for someone to notice and exclaim, "They were born in different years! Identical twins, and they'll never have the same birthday!"

Now, it wasn't as though Campbell forced this story on people. It came up naturally. (One thing twins learn early is that, for the rest of their lives, people *are* going to ask, "Which one of you is older?") Campbell would try to get away with saying that they were born on New Year's Eve and leave it at that. Or she would try to tell the funny bits, about how furious she got at Tim for ignoring her and watching the shimmering ball above Times Square on TV, as well as admiring women in the crowd who were dressed up in copies of early-twentieth-century finery (since the movie everyone was watching that year was *Titanic*).

At the hospital, as the moment of the birth grew closer, Tim looked up at the TV and said, "We could go there someday. Don't you think it would be fun? Think about next year and how beautiful you'd look in one of those low-cut dresses. Or we could go there when the twins are three. For the new millennium. Would you like that?"

And Campbell, her face as red and swollen as a cartoon chipmunk's, said, "I would like it. I would like it even more if you fell off a cliff."

She told the nurses that they had planned to name the girls Andrea and Arden. But moments after their birth, Tim heard Campbell say, "Hush, little Meredith. There, there, Mallory." And barely had he opened his mouth to object when Campbell snapped, "I know what we *planned*. But when you give birth to two babies in two minutes, you can name them Batman and Robin if you want. *Their* names are Meredith and Mallory!"

Campbell never forgot to mention that, technically, the girls were born in different years. It made them unique—and if Campbell wanted anything, it was never to diminish the twins' uniqueness. At least as far as their mother knew, they had little enough of that to begin with—certainly when they were small.

But even before they were born, the babies knew how it was to be completely bonded and completely opposite. Meredith was happy by basic nature. She would always love pretty things, pretty people, and hopeful solutions. Mallory was intense and would always worry, even when she didn't need to. She would look at questions in complicated ways and refuse to accept the easy answer. Merry would attract friends the way Velcro picks up tennis balls, while Mallory, unless she was playing sports, would spend most of her time with her sister or else alone by choice. Before they came into the great world, she was the baby content to float in the warm dark seas, examining her fingertips and stroking her cheek, trying to figure out what being a person meant. Meredith wanted to feel and find everything. Side to side and up and down she zoomed, like a mermaid in flight. All that zooming got on Mallory's nerves as months passed, and the quarters got closer in there. She sometimes put out a tiny hand to slow her sister down. And Meredith always responded. At Mallory's touch she settled down and, entwined, head to foot, they would drift into sleep, as the voices from outside slipped into their dreams.

These voices were ones they grew to recognize, as they bloomed from pink buds to babies fully formed—with fingers and toes and personalities—separated only by a wall of muscle from the great world all around them. They heard the voice of their mother, giving and taking orders all day, a quick, light, practical note in a room where the beeping and whooshing and clanging were the music. There was their father—friendly and loud, but also protective and calm. There was the voice of their grandmother, a soft voice that always alerted the babies to listen closely, even before they were born.

One day, the twins listened as Gwenny told her daughter-in-law that both babies were girls. Much as she loved her mother-in-law, Campbell was annoyed. Like any new mother—or at least most of them—she wanted the surprise. So her voice was sharper than she meant it to be when she asked just how her mother-in-law knew the babies' gender and why she considered this so important. Yes, she knew that all the women in her husband's family *supposedly* had "the sight." But at least back then, Campbell thought that "the sight" was a bunch of baloney. And so Gwenny's prediction was just a lucky guess. Campbell wiggled her foot with impatience. She wished that Gwenny would get on with it.

"Well, they're both girls. So they're probably identical twins. Identical twin girls run in our family," Gwenny said. "I thought you should be ready. Twins are different from other babies. And not just because there are two of them. They're joined. Not joined like kids who are born sharing a hip or a rib. Joined by the spirit."

Campbell still didn't get why this was such a big deal. She'd read up on identical twins, in several authoritative books from the library. What Gwenny seemed to want to tell her was something else, something more; but she didn't say anything else, or anything more. Finally Campbell decided that Gwenny was being unnecessarily dramatic. Being dramatic seemed to run in her husband's family, too. The baby twins sensed, however, not with words but with feelings, that what Gwenny said about their being inseparable was important.

And they were inseparable.

After they were born, for example, they fretted and sobbed in their sweet little cradles. Meredith couldn't bear to be away from Mallory. Mallory was cranky and tense if she couldn't see her twin. Their mother finally decided to ignore the experts' advice.

Weary to the ends of her fingers, she put them together in one cradle next to their parents' big bed. From then on, she found them each morning, one right side up and one upside down, each clasping the other's tiny foot. At precisely the same moments, throughout the night, they made precisely the same sounds—chirping and cooing—turning over at precisely the same time. They never woke up for feeding, though they drained Campbell during the day. She didn't realize it, but she had given them what they wanted most of all. They needed nothing, not even food, more than they needed each other. In fact, on the night they were born, Meredith, as excitable and bouncy in the world as she had been before she arrived, wriggled and shuddered with angry, piercing cries the moment she slid with a smack into the doctor's hands. The huge, cold new place was bad enough. Being alone—without her other—was even worse. The doctor was just glad that this baby was a live wire, because twins who came early could be tiny and in trouble. But the first baby girl grew calm as soon as her sister arrived, just two minutes later, quietly gazing around her and breathing slowly on her own. He couldn't have known why. Without being able to speak aloud, Mallory and Meredith were already speaking to each other in what would become their private language. Mallory thought her way to Meredith. *Soso,* Mallory thought to her sobbing twin. *Soso . . . don't cry. Everything is all right.* Meredith heard and quieted down. It would always be "soso," a word that meant nothing to anyone but to them. *Soso . . . don't cry. Siow . . . I'm scared. I'm hurt.*

Bonnie Jellico, who had never witnessed twins born in such a short time except through a surgery, remembered thinking it was like seeing two copies glide out of the portal of a copy machine. They were beautiful, with thick black hair and softly pointed chins.

But they weren't copies.

When they looked at each other, they saw what other people see when they look into a mirror.

It would be years before anyone except their mother noticed that Meredith was right-handed, while Mallory held her spoon with her left hand. Merry's straight, silky hair parted on the right, Mally's on the left. The family also assumed that as they grew, they would have similar personalities but spend more time apart.

Instead, they had dissimilar personalities but refused to spend more time apart: Merry even came home from sleepovers before breakfast. That was only one of many things people assumed about them—and which, like the others, was wrong.

When they were three, Grandfather Arness, their mother's father, built them matching youth beds. On one headboard they pasted all their cartoon and holiday stickers and made their first attempts to write their names in crayon. After they fell asleep each night, Campbell tried moving one of them back into the unused bed. Though she didn't scream as though she were being dissected, the way she had when she was born, Merry couldn't be at rest until she was with Mallory, or at least knew that Mallory was nearby and okay. Outgoing Merry, happiest surrounded by all kinds of people, dancing when she could have walked and jabbering before she thought about what to say, seemed to be the natural "leader." In fact, Meredith always waited, especially on important matters, to see what Mallory would do or say. It was she who was the clingy one, who crept every night into Mally's bed—until they grew so big that they literally had no room to turn over without kicking the other onto the floor.

But that took years, because neither of them got very big, ever.

Their mother listened to their language and tried to learn what the words meant.

"Soso," they told each other—and Campbell translated this to mean *"Everything is fine. Don't cry."*

"Laybite," they told each other when one twin needed the other to stop talking—right that very minute.

But even as closely as she studied them, their mother couldn't quite believe how often they didn't need words at all.

She never knew that when one looked at the sky, or sprained her ankle, the other saw the star or winced at the pain. When they grew older, if one wanted to kiss a boy, the other felt the longing, even if she didn't like the boy.

As the years passed, and Campbell felt sure that the girls talked to each other with their minds, she didn't tell anyone, not even Tim. Of course Tim knew, too, or thought he did, but he didn't tell Campbell. Campbell didn't want to upset Tim. Tim didn't want Campbell to worry. He was used to twin ways. Both his mother and his grandmother were twins.

The night Mallory and Merry were born, Grandma Gwenny couldn't even wait until morning to see them. Their grandfather assumed that Gwen had to go running out into the snow (wouldn't catch *him* doing that!) because she was finally a grandmother. But the reason was bigger than that. Gwenny crept into the room and kissed her son, Tim, who was asleep in a big chair with a hat that read "Super Male" over his eyes. Then she tiptoed over to Campbell's side, hoping not to wake her or the babies, hoping just for a glimpse.

But Campbell had just finished feeding the girls. She felt shriveled as a raisin but happy to see Gwenny's eager face.

"Don't you know how to celebrate New Year's Eve!" said Gwenny, shaking her finger at Campbell.

"They're pretty cute. And I'm pretty overwhelmed already," Campbell said with a sigh. "Well, at least we've got our whole family, all in one night."

"No, I think . . . well, I know that you'll have a little boy," Gwenny said.

Campbell wrinkled her nose. There went Gwenny with her visions again.

"And you'll be glad because identical twins are . . . they're one person. You remember what I said that time. They'll be closer to each other than anyone else, even closer than they are to you."

How awful, Campbell thought.

She tried to smile, but had to bite her lip to stop it from trembling. Exhausted, and having just met two people she already loved more than her own life, she didn't want to hear that she would never be as dear to them as other mothers were to *their* daughters. But she listened—and took a moment to reflect on just why—because something about Gwenny seemed so sad and yearning underneath the happiness. Gwenny sat down on the windowsill and gazed out at the veil of snow. "Isn't snow beautiful? But so treacherous, especially on a night like this with people swerving around like fools. We're probably the safest people in Ridgeline right here. But you can't deny that there's something magical about snow."

A scattering of little thoughts coalesced into a tiny whirlwind in Campbell's mind. Her mother-in-law wasn't thinking only of snow, or of her new grandchildren. Gwenny, she remembered, had been an identical twin, whose sister had died as a child. No one talked about the accident. After that night, for the rest of her life, Campbell would be able to picture the grief on Gwenny's beautiful unlined face in profile, by the light from the window. How painful it still was for Gwenny, after fifty years, to be without her . . . other. *Other?* Campbell thought. What did that mean?

The babies, nearly asleep, heard Campbell thinking and were happy that their mother was smart.

But there was more to Gwenny's stew of emotions than even Campbell knew.

She had to confess that she nearly hoped that these little girls would be regular kids, unusual only because they were twins—not in the strange, painful, potent, almost unbearable way Gwenny knew so well. But she sensed that they were, and confirmed that for herself the first time she looked into their round, curious, river-colored eyes. As proud as she was of her heritage, as much as she knew that the gift was important—to her, and if God gave it, she supposed, important altogether—it was a two-hearted bequest, a blessing with a sharp bite. If only she could explain to them what life held for them, in a way that would spare them fear or pain. But she couldn't. She didn't know, for certain, what the nature of their gift would be. She could not have guessed its supremacy over all the twins in previous generations of the Brynn family. But she did know that the little girls would never put faith in what they needed to know unless they learned the old and cruel way—on their own.

Four and a half years later, Campbell sat on a bench next to the cold ashes of the fire pit, her arms wrapped tightly around her two-year-old son, Adam.

Police swarmed the woods and clearings surrounding the Brynn family's cabin camp, some restraining great wolf like dogs on leather leashes.

She had not watched Meredith closely enough. Meredith was dreamy and creative and liked to wander. So long as she held hands mentally with Mallory, she thought she was safe. Someone said that Merry had followed a deer and twin fawns down the hiking path two hours earlier. The sun hadn't quite set then, and now darkness was closing in. She was such a little girl, and these woods and hills so vast, the cliffs above the river so steep.

Campbell thought she would like to die that instant. She blamed herself.

Mallory sat nearby on the grass with her back to her mother, playing with a shell necklace. Tim's aunt had given the girls the necklaces, identical except for the colors, earlier in the spring. Mallory's lips were moving as she twirled the shells, but she made no sound that Campbell could hear. Unless she spoke to Mallory, Mallory wouldn't say a thing, Campbell knew. Not for the second or third or fiftieth time, Campbell thought of Gwenny's words on the night her daughters were born, about twins being one person. After a while, Campbell asked, softly, "Are you . . . talking to Merry?"

Mallory, absorbed, didn't answer. Campbell asked again.

"Laybite," she said softly. Campbell knew this meant, in twin code, something about the need to be quiet.

"Mallory?" Campbell asked again. "Are you talking to Merry?"

Briefly, but with an effort, Mallory answered, "Yes, Mommy."

"Did you tell her to stand still and not be afraid of the big doggies?"

"Yes, Mommy."

"Mally, do you know where she is? Is she afraid?"

"No, she's not afraid," Mally said. "I'm talking her, so she knows the doggies will come." When Mally was upset, she slipped back into the kind of sentences she'd used when she was three. "By the water drops. Soso. Soso."

"So what?" Campbell asked, forgetting a twin word she *did* know. "Are you sure you don't mean down by the pond in the middle of the river?" Campbell asked, as she had half a dozen times before, her skin tightening with the fear she felt of the slippery, sucking mud on the riverbank. Meredith and Mallory could swim, but just, like puppies. "Is Merry at the river?"

"*No*, Mommy," Mallory said sharply, dragging her eyes up to meet Campbell's. "I told you. The water drops. Not the swimming hole."

"Rain?"

"Mommy!" Mallory snapped, suddenly angry. She had always been the more volatile, Merry the more . . . well, merry. Campbell felt a total fool, gingerly trying to avoid riling up a kindergarten child.

"Just stop you!" Mally cried out.

Campbell glanced around to see if Tim or his sisters and any of the cousins and their spouses, or his ancient aunties, had noticed Mallory's outburst. Tim and his father and brothers, compelled by some ancient law of being men, were out following the police, probably messing up the dogs' scent trails, Campbell thought in a moment of spite. The women remained behind, helplessly making and drinking gallons of coffee.

Campbell thought that the theory of relativity had never been better illustrated. Every minute was only sixty seconds long, but it stretched out like bubble gum until it sagged and tore and then it stretched again. Besides Campbell, only her mother-in-law, seated lightly on the arm of one of the big swings, never moved. She watched Campbell with an unwavering gaze of pity—though she did not venture closer. Campbell supposed that she was thinking about her own twin as well as her granddaughter.

Campbell didn't want to know what her mother-in-law was thinking.

A half hour passed.

When Campbell glanced at her watch again, another three minutes had expired.

Suddenly then, Campbell heard the shouts from the woods: "We found her!" and "She's fine! We've got her!"

She noticed, with a helpless sadness—how could poor Adam ever understand this?—she had actually gripped her little boy's wrists so tightly, she had left red finger marks on his skin. Then she let herself take a full breath and began to cry for the first time since Meredith had disappeared.

A burly older officer carried Merry out of the woods and set her down. She ran toward Campbell's open arms . . . and straight to Mally.

"Did you watch water?" Mally asked, reaching out to pull a burr from Meredith's thick, shining, black bobbed hair that swung just above her shoulders. Mallory's hair was short, swept back in a feathery cap.

"Beester!" Meredith said. "I watched so long!" Merry then reached up and patted Mallory's face, as though she, Merry, were blind. To Campbell's astonishment, Mallory began touching her sister's elbows and wrists, then her knees, watching Merry's face for a reaction. She was feeling for broken bones . . . she was making sure that Meredith was not hurt.

Out of breath from having jogged half a mile back on the pebbled trail down the ridge with his little bundle, the police officer finally caught up and said, "She was sitting still as a mouse, ma'am. Did you teach her to always sit still if she ever got lost? That was wise. She was watching a crack in a rock with the tiniest little—"

"Waterfall," Campbell said, pulling Merry back into her lap, holding her close, inhaling the heavy scent of pine that rose from her daughter's sweet head. "Thank you. Thank you so much."

"Exactly," the heavyset officer continued. "You know the place, then."

"Her sister knows," Campbell told him. She smiled across the yard at her mother-in-law as the relatives swept forward. The older woman nodded, the fingers of both her hands lifted, the fingertips meeting at her lips in a kiss.

THE LAST BEST NIGHT

THE LAST BEST NIGHT

Two nights before New Year's Day, which would be her thirteenth birthday, Mallory Brynn was certain that she died
before she could wake.

The burning golden panel of cloth fell on her like a great web,
sealing her in a searing cocoon. When she tried to breathe, the
filaments and sizzling threads of the fabric scorched her throat.
Her lungs collapsed into charred, useless flaps. Her last thoughts
were of Adam, so little, and her younger cousins. She was sure
that Meredith had gotten out with them in time. . . .

"Sit up!" Meredith shouted. Mallory mumbled, her hands flail-
ing, still fighting the dream. "Mally!" Meredith said again. "I've
tried to wake you up three times! Could you *be* more limp? Do
you really want to sleep through your own birthday party?"

"Oh my God!" Mally whispered, sitting up and pinching her
forearms to verify that she was still flesh and bone and not ash. "I

forgot all about it. I had the most horrible dream! I dreamed I died in a fire, Merry. I dreamed I was dead."

"You were out of it like you were dead, Mallory! I hate when you go random like this. You just don't care."

"I'm tired from practice," Mallory, who played indoor soccer in the off-season, said. She pulled off her socks and added, "Plus, I hate parties."

She did not, but she was so deeply shy that being introduced was, for her, like being scraped with the tines of a fork.

"You hate parties? How can we be related?"

"I just . . . don't know what to say. I can't say, 'Oh, Alli's wearing white and so is Crystal. How totally dorky, hanging with the trendies,' " Mally simpered in what she considered a good imitation of her sister's friends.

"My friends don't talk like that."

"They do so."

"So do yours."

"I don't have any friends like that," Mallory said.

Merry realized, with a pang of sympathy, that this was true. Now that they were in junior high, boys didn't want to hang with Mally for the same reasons she *still* wanted to hang with them. Mallory's best friends were high-school girls from the Eighty-Niners, the traveling soccer squad. They liked her enough. But there was no such thing as a high-school girl who would want to sleep over with a thirteen-year-old if she wasn't babysitting her.

"Well, when you see people, just say, 'Thanks for the present,' "

Merry said, soldiering on. "Say, 'Thanks for coming.' Are you stupid or something?"

"We told them not to bring presents."

"But nobody pays attention to that. They'll bring some anyway," Meredith said hopefully, examining her reflection in the long mirror their father had glued to the back of their door. Her blunt-cut black hair shone like a new boot. A box-pleated melon miniskirt, the light wool tweed crisscrossed with pale blue strands, worn over white tights, topped off by a cami and a man's blue twill cuffed shirt, matched her alternating white-and-melon fingertips and toes perfectly. She sighed in hard-earned pleasure. It had taken four hours at the Deptford Mall—an expedition that would have excited Mallory as much as shopping for batteries. But the effect was worth it—casual, not too on-purpose, dressed up a little bit by the three matching pearl studs their parents had given each girl. Their mother had pierced their ears—taking care to put two holes in Mallory's left ear and two in Meredith's right ear—to tell them apart. A trio of tiny, perfect pearl studs was their parents' present to each girl.

When the girls turned out to be mirror twins, and the piercings corresponded to the correct side for each girl, Campbell was astonished. When she'd chosen the spots for the piercings, she'd had no idea.

Merry wondered for a moment if she should ditch her pearls for her white-bead chandeliers. But that would hurt their parents' feelings.

Mally was wearing *her* pearls. That was at least a start.

So Meredith ransacked her sister's closet. There were only two remotely possible shirts. The best hope was a cream-colored thing with a hint of a ruffle at the shoulders. It was clearly meant for summer, but Mally could throw it over a long-sleeved tee, if Mally *had* a tee that didn't look as if it had gone under the lawn mower. Meredith could lend her a real silk gray turtleneck, but she would spend the whole night watching Mally like a hawk. Mally was *such* a slob. She threw herself around like an eleven-year-old guy—still! She wore hockey skates! She *rode her bike* to school in nice weather, to Meredith's utter humiliation. She slept in Bugs Bunny boxers. Mally's definition of "dressed up" was wearing something she hadn't already worn twice—in the same week! And still, all she had to do was brush her hair and zip! Mallory was as beautiful as Merry, except that for Merry it was a full-time job.

Merry was too young to have any idea that all the washing grains and crunches she inflicted on herself were unnecessary—that both girls' basic elfin cuteness was genetic. She liked seeing herself as a slave to her appearance. It justified how much she spent on things just because she liked how they smelled. It justified the hours she spent simply stroking her soft, textured garments, nearly in tears because they were so beautiful and they would last long after she, Merry, got old and died. She would never have considered it a selfish thing that she locked the box where she kept her jewelry or crossed elastic bands over the front of the shelves where she stored her sweaters, folded in order not just by color but by shade.

She wanted to forbid people to touch her things, but couldn't bear to admit it. It was at odds with her generally sentimental and loving self—about which she was also vain.

Finally, knowing it would be wrong to let her twin go down to the party looking like a homeless person, she pulled down her silky turtleneck, the color of moonlight on a summer lawn, trying to put the picture of it with a mustard stain on the middle out of her mind.

"Here, Mal," Merry said. "You can wear this under your nice cream blouse. . . ."

"I hate that blouse. It's too tight!"

"It's supposed to be tight, duh! It's supposed to show you have a waist!"

Mally grumbled as she rolled out of bed and headed for the shower. "I barely do have a waist."

This was true. At four feet and ten inches, neither of the girls had yet what would be termed "figures."

Meredith did her best to cinch in at the middle what basically went straight up and back down. Despite the personal distinction she made between herself, a cheerleader, and her sister, a jock, Merry also was a committed and agile athlete. Only eighty-eight pounds, she was the team's cocaptain and a "flyer," tossed five feet into the air above the gymnasium floor to land in a basket catch, lifted on the thighs and shoulders of bigger girls of the pyramid.

Mallory emerged from the shower with wet hair and an alarmed expression.

"Why did you have to invite guys?" she asked. "Everyone thinks I'm an idiot. I probably dreamed I was on fire because of unconscious free-floating anxiety or something."

"Free-floating what? They're not sleeping over! And no one thinks you're an idiot," Meredith explained. "How could they? You never say anything. They probably just think you're gay."

"Maybe I am gay."

"Well, then dress up for the girls. Jeez, Mal. You're trying to drive me crazy," Meredith finally said, spinning Mallory around, tucking and fussing. "And it's working. Stand up straight!"

"Ugh," Mallory said, and flicked at the ruffles that flattered her strong, broad shoulders. She stood up straight and her natural grace took over. "I look like crap. I wish I was wearing a tracksuit."

"You look *normal*, Mal. You're not used to normal. Most people don't wear gym shorts in December with T-shirts that have stupid graffiti jokes on them."

"I love my shirts! Drew gave me those shirts." The girls' next-door neighbor was a boy three years older, but had grown up with the twins. When Drew's mother, Hilary, wanted to torment them, she brought out photos of all three of them wearing diapers and nothing else. Now, Drew had a special place in their hearts because he had recently acquired both his older sister's Toyota truck and his driver's license.

"He gave them to you *after* he wore them until they were too small!" Merry snapped.

"That's what I think was so sweet," Mallory replied in Drew's defense.

"They have sweat stains on the pits!" Merry sneered.

"Big deal. I wear them to sleep in! What's wrong with sweat?" Mallory used their ancient language to warn Merry to stop talking. "Laybite!"

After a long, tense pause, Merry said with a sigh, "Listen, Mallory. I'll shut up in a minute. People have been planning for this for weeks."

A hundred kids had been invited by e-mail, most of them eighth graders and freshmen. But Drew, still a steadfast friend, especially to Mallory, despite the great divide that had opened between them two years before when Drew went to high school, was bringing at least six of his cross-country teammates. Who knew who else might hear about the party and show up to affect nonchalance? Maybe her best friend Kim's older brother, David!

Merry shivered with excitement over this fact alone.

"Mally, just make an appearance," Merry pleaded. "Pretend you're going to have fun. It's my birthday, too, and you have no right to make me feel guilty for being excited."

"Of course. It's all about you, Merry."

"Well, if you sit up here, people all over town are going to think you're a mutant or something! No one misses her own birthday party. It'll be all over town tomorrow."

In this she was correct. In Ridgeline, population 1,501, everyone knew the Brynn twins.

If they didn't know the twins to speak to, they'd seen their soccer and cheerleading photos—from the first grade to last year's snapshots—displayed on the wall behind the counter at Domino Sporting Goods, the store Tim owned with his best friend, Rick Domini. Everyone in town passed through Domino Sports, to buy backyard tetherballs and knee braces and hockey sticks and team uniforms and running shoes—although the Target out by the

Deptford Mall was cheaper. Loyalty made them spend the extra dollar or three—that, and the confidence that came from Tim's amiable ability to remember to ask about their trick knees or shin splints.

People liked making the Saturday morning circuit around Ridgeline's brick-paved town square. It hadn't changed in any essential way for 160 years.

The Mountain Beanery Coffee Shop had replaced the dressmaker, and the Ridge State Bank had taken over Helmsley's Funeral Home. (People still saw this as a fair exchange and made jokes about it.) When Miss Alice's daughter, Jenny, took over Miss Alice's Dance and made it into Jenny's Leap Beyond and Fitness Fit for You, she built her own little square studio out near the middle school, making way for Open Sesame, the Greenbergs' bagel bakery and deli.

In the middle of the square was a larger-than-life-size bronze that people had seen all their lives but which few understood. A woman in a long, sweeping cloak held two children's faces against her skirts. Although it was called *Courage*, the statue depicted the widow of one of the miners who died ninety years before when a shaft collapsed in a copper vein up off Canada Road. Out from the square, like four spokes, the four arteries—Main Street, Pilgrim Road, School Street, and Cemetery Road—led to the places anyone might imagine and a few that no one would.

Main Street got most of the traffic. It went to the big concrete loop that formed the entrance to the highway into New York City, one hundred miles away. If people went straight, past the highway overpass, eventually they came to the Deptford Mall and Cinema. School Street passed all six area schools—the elementary, the middle school, the two public high schools, Saint Francis of Assisi, and Ridgeford Community College.

By contrast, Pilgrim Road was barely traveled—and to the annoyance of its residents, only sporadically plowed. Just a few blocks out were the big, three-story clapboard homes that had been farmhouses before Ridgeline was a proper town. In one of them, Tim and Campbell Brynn lived with their family.

When they fell from ladders, or popped hernias, needed hips replaced or benign tumors excised, when they had babies that wouldn't come the regular way or children whose inflamed tonsils kept them coughing and smelling of VapoRub all winter long, the people of Ridgeline met Campbell . . . usually first as a pair of whimsical blue eyes between the rim of her surgical hairnet and the top of her face mask. She was tender and efficient when they fell asleep frightened, cheerful and solicitous when they awoke in pain.

Her girls were a local landmark. Everyone told the tale of their birth to friends from out of town, if they got around to it, like the story of the hurricane that passed through twenty years before and didn't destroy one single house but did drive an egg into the trunk of a tree without breaking the shell. Never gave their parents a day's trouble, neighbors said of the twins—although Campbell would have disputed that point. The twins and their ten-year-old brother, Adam, had never, so far as any of them knew, had an argument of substance with anyone except Drew.

And those were sacred and planned rituals.

For him, the twins regularly devised tortures, as if he were still their old playmate on the wooden swing set. They waited until he was parked in the driveway with a date and then dumped a twenty-pound bag of birdseed from their bedroom window onto the roof of his car. Then, patiently as a sibling, Drew waited until the right moment to exact his revenge, with an amiable determination. Color copies of Merry with cucumber slices over her eyes, sunbathing behind the garage in her little brother's boxers with the Sunday comics spread over her chest, were taped to dozens of the lockers at her school. Mallory's new Australian fleecy boots, left outside her back door to dry, had cherry tomatoes tucked in the toes.

The Brynns were not unlike most families in Ridgeline.

There were fewer divorces than the New York State norm, but the town had its share of single moms. Even in most of the two-parent families, both parents worked. The usual number of children was three instead of two. The Methodist and Presbyterian churches faced each other squarely on corners of the same street. Most kids knew how to skate by the age of three and to ski by the age of five, and even men whose sons had moved to Seattle still turned out for the Friday night football games. The copper mines were gone now, but the copper remained, tinting the soil up in the hills with a sparkly grit. The copper miners were gone, too. But they had left behind large families. In the cemetery, the same names that repeated along ranks of headstones—Morgan, Vaughan, Massenger—still showed up on the athletic plaques at school and the dentists' shingle at the medical center.

At its best, Ridgeline was like a family, defending the eccentricities of its elders and generally embracing newcomers who made an effort to put down serious roots. At its worst, it was like a family, withholding approval, trading speculation and gossip, feuding and forgiving. Like a family, at holidays and funerals, weddings and graduations, they gathered to mourn and to celebrate. Fully a tenth of them or more gathered that Friday night to wish the twins a happy passage to the next plateau of their lives.

That Mallory was being such a mule was made even worse by the fact that they would be spending their *real* birthday—New Year's Eve—babysitting their brother *and* their three younger cousins.

Campbell had laid down the law. "Dad and I have waited for years to go to New York for New Year's Eve. You're needed when you're needed. And I'm certainly not going to pay a babysitter when I have you two, especially not after throwing you a big birthday bash. So lose the long face, Meredith. Mallory's taking it okay."

"Mallory has no life," Merry had protested, and got nowhere.

Now, Merry tried a new tack. "Mal, you're never going to get a guy. . . ." she said.

"I told you. I don't want to get a guy! Not yet. Not *this week*! It would be . . . like having a job. You know, you have to call them all the time and they have to call you. Look at you and Will Brent. You were supposedly 'going out' all last year. You couldn't even go to the movies. You're not allowed. You hung around at the mall and held hands. Why would I want to do that? And David, your big crush, he thinks you're a little baby on a Big Wheels."

In the midst of her rant, Mallory thought fleetingly of Drew. She loved Drew, and sometimes her feelings for him were confused. He was her buddy; if Drew came to the door to borrow something or pick them up to drive them to school, and Mally was in her pajamas, she didn't feel the need to scream and run upstairs. But sometimes, when Drew grinned and tickled her . . . she felt something else. . . .

She was about to tell Meredith that when Meredith purred, "Let's see how David feels next year, when I'm in high school."

David Jellico was the older brother of Merry's best friend, who was, in turn, the daughter of their mother's best friend, Bonnie. Merry often explained to Mallory that it would just be perfect if she and David grew up and got married because their mothers could be in-laws. David, she prattled on until Mally wanted to scream, was not just cute, like most guys, but truly beautiful, with his perfect nose and slightly olive skin and long blond thatch. Merry thought David's face looked like something traced from a history book, like a face from a Roman myth. Mallory thought Merry was nuts. She considered David Jellico, with his sweaters tied around his neck like he'd just jumped off a yacht, too much like a boy model to be even semi-interesting.

She also knew that she could beat him in a race, any day of the week.

But now, Mallory smiled reluctantly at her sister. *Oh well. She's Merry.* Being at the center of a giggling crowd, like a chick surrounded by big peacocks, was Merry's idea of heaven. She *liked* it when boys picked her up and held her like a life-size doll; she liked actually wearing a size zero—like the puking girls, but without puking.

On the other hand, any boy who tried to pick Mallory up like a toy would have faced serious damage to his kneecaps. When Drew told her that legally, she was a midget—as if there were a legal definition for midgetness, as there was for blindness—she popped a bubble from her customary huge wad of gum in his face.

Despite her devotion to sports, Mallory was still heroically lazy, happiest on the sofa with a ginger ale and a whole tower of saltines for three straight hours of recorded soap operas.

"How can you stand watching old people talking about sex?" Merry would ask. "How can you stand the creepy hairstyles?"

"They comfort me," Mally answered. "They're like life. Nobody ever talks about anything that matters in real life, either. Like in school. All just a bunch of lies and temper tantrums. Look at you and Kim. And I like that when it's Halloween on the soaps, it's Halloween in real life. It's very fishbowl." If she ran out of soaps, Mally watched science fiction and mystery movies of every description that were old when their mother was their age. She owned stacks of old tapes she had lugged home from garage sales on her bike, along with the last VCR made in America. Mallory pulled that home in a *wagon*. Meredith was glad the only one who saw her was Drew, who yelled, "You need some green canvas sneakers and geraniums, Brynn. You look like my grandma Shirley going around the square at the Farmers' Market!"

Unperturbed, Mallory set up the cruddy old thing in the living room.

Merry would come into the house with Kim, and Mallory would hold up her hand in the darkness. "Movie," she would say. "No idiot speak." Mallory was as rude as a guy.

No one, not even Kim, quite "got" the twins. She and her own brother were nowhere near as loyal as Meredith and Mally were. They made fun of each other, but Kim was sure that Mallory would kill anyone who tried to hurt Merry. She hoped David would do the same for her.

"Mally, come on!" Merry pleaded. Mallory didn't stir. If anything, she curled tighter into herself. Then finally, for the first time that night, Merry took a long look at Mally's face.

Mallory looked lousy, pasty-faced, her big gray-blue eyes darkened, troubled, like puddles muddied by a rainstorm. It wasn't the party, the clothes, or the boys. "Anno," Merry said—old twin language that meant "*I care that you hurt. I'm here. You're not hurting alone.*" "Tell me."

In a rush, Mally said, "I dreamed that we were in a fire and these burning window drapes fell on me and I suffocated. I woke up totally covered in sweat. I've never had a dream like that. Aren't you supposed to really *die* if you dream you die?"

"That's an old wives' tale," Meredith said, feeling that same creep of fear. "It's just nerves."

"It didn't feel like an old wives' tale," Mallory went on, as Meredith slowly got up and began to blow out her twin's thick black thatch of hair, so that the ends flipped under and lay against

Mallory's cheeks. Mally continued, "I should hate your guts. You didn't even ask me about my dream. . . ."

I didn't want to, Merry thought. It wasn't just that she didn't have the time. There was a foreboding for her in hearing this, like seeing ambulance lights revolve in the distance. Merry was trying hard not to absorb her sister's misery.

"Just try to let go of it," Merry advised. "You're overreacting."

They could hear the doorbell pealing. The party was set up in the garage, which Tim Brynn built with heat pipes when he added it on to the three-story saltbox where Brynn relatives had lived for four generations—mostly so he could use his workshop year-round. Before they moved to their ranch, Tim's parents had lived in the house, raising their children there. His grandfather, Walker, lived there before then, and his great-grandfather before that. Now, every bike and sled, as well as the library ladder that Adam and Tim hadn't quite finished in time for Campbell's Christmas present, was stacked outside and placed under a tarp against the dim possibility of snow. Tim had stocked his pride and joy, a fifties soda machine, with Cokes and Orange Crush, and a long table wobbled under the weight of hot dogs, salsa, chips, dip, and a cake that was half white, half chocolate (Mallory hated chocolate). Tim's iPod, in its dock of tiny, powerful speakers, was secured on a makeshift shelf far out of anyone's reach. Campbell was elated. She had earlier called their efforts a "winter wonderland."

But that was only in the Brynns' garage.

To the disgust of everyone in Ridgeline, there hadn't been even a halfhearted flake of snow since Halloween. The winter was open and dry, after a bitter and prolonged fall. But tinsel and banners draped the walls, and Campbell had raided both fabric stores at the mall for all the white and silver tulle she could scrounge, to make it as festive inside as it was dreary outside.

And now, Meredith could hear *David's* voice downstairs. He was dropping Kim off, but how long would he stay? David had to see her in her melon skirt!

"Come on, Ster," she said softly, hugging Mally, using their baby name for each other, the one Adam still used for both of them. "It was a bad dream, but it was just a dream."

"I'm not going to talk about it all night, if that's what you're worried about," Mallory said. Merry jumped. She had been worrying—about just that very thing.

"I don't want you to *think* about it all night," Merry answered. Since she could feel Mallory's thoughts, that would be just as awful. "Why worry about something that didn't happen? Forget it."

"That's your answer to everything," Mally griped.

"It works for me!"

"You didn't feel it!" Mally paused and asked, "Hey, why didn't you feel it?"

Why hadn't she? Merry set down the blow-dryer.

When Mallory was knocked flat by an overzealous opponent on the soccer field, Merry, miles away at the mall, had to catch her breath. When Merry started to sweat from nerves before a math quiz, Mally's palms got sticky. There was nothing eerie about this. They expected it. It was as ordinary to them as Mallory thinking about the right answer to the story problem and Merry writing it down, or Merry defining "cacophony" in her head so that Mally could pass her vocab test. It was like their twin language—so elaborate it included past tenses and the names of everyone in the family, in translation. Their brother Adam was "Liba," which the twins supposed was a toddler term for "little baby." They could figure out the toddler derivation of "siow," which meant "I'm hurt." But they had no memory of beginning to speak their language. It was as if they'd received it, fully formed, like a book of poems they were expected to memorize.

In the same way, dreaming the same dreams at the same time was the usual: Their father had watched them in their sleep when they were tiny, one girl talking in her sleep about losing her stuffed poodle, the other asking if she'd found it.

What was creepy was that there was a dream now that only one of them knew about.

"If I dreamed it, why didn't you?" Mally asked again.

"Because . . . because . . . probably because I was *awake*," Meredith explained, after a pause. She was improvising, and Mally knew it. A little spool of nausea began to unwind in her belly. She should have heard Mally's dream, or felt it. Still, Mally's moods were going to give *Merry* an ulcer. "Can we please go downstairs now? We can obsess later on. Otherwise, I'm going without you. I've got to dance."

Mallory ignored her.

"Mal," Merry said after a moment, "this is me." She began to dance as if the closet door mirror were a cute guy, glancing up at him from under her long eyelashes, then switching her lead and tossing her hair back over her shoulder. Then she stuck out her stomach and rounded her shoulders. "This is you."

At last, Mallory laughed.

She jumped up, perused her actually-pretty-decent reflection, and clattered down the back stairs. They made a grand entrance under the arch Tim had wound with hundreds of white twinkle lights. Even David Jellico seemed to notice.

And it was that kind of night, a night like ten thousand twinkle lights—the best fun the twins would have . . . to be honest, they told each other later when they talked about it, ever again in their lives.

The party would be the last time that they didn't know what they didn't know—the thing for which Mally's horrifying dream was only the opening note.

As time passed, thirteen years of not knowing would seem a kind of blessing. Mallory would often remind Merry that *she* hadn't really wanted to turn thirteen. Something about it nagged at her. She figured she simply was still too happy to be a kid, not really ready to be an official teenager. But after they knew the real reason, even Merry would mourn all the days she spent so freely, unburdened by awareness, and wish she had treasured them.

At the party that night, Mally got over her fear of guys long enough to dance with Justin Springer, Dane Greenberg, and Daniel Eppelin. She smiled, showing the dimple in her left cheek, all but flirting with everybody.

"Daniel likes you," Merry told her, showing the dimple in her right cheek. "He looks all mushed."

"Merry, be real. We danced, like, twice," Mally said. "It's not like a big romance."

"It's good enough," Merry said, who got her first kiss that night, from Will Brent—who was trying hard to win her back and almost succeeding. But she also got a crashing headache, as if Mally's dream had passed to her like a virus.

Generally, though, it was a great party, although most people wouldn't think of it that way. They would remember only that they'd seen the twins just two nights before the fire.

UNLUCKY THIRTEEN

UNLUCKY THIRTEEN

"You have Auntie Karin's cell number," Campbell reminded them for the hundredth time as the family piled into the van. Dutifully, Merry fished the list out of her pocket and held it up, rolling her eyes. "And Mallory, you brought the nice video games for the little kids, and the party hats? I want them all in bed by nine thirty, but you can have them watch the New Year—"

"On TV, at seven p.m. from London," Mally repeated. "Mom! You've told us all this so many times I could write a song about it! We know what to do!"

It was five p.m., barely dark, as they set out down Pilgrim and out Cemetery Road.

Cemetery Road curved up toward Mountain Rest Cemetery. At a respectful distance, the ancient cemetery now overlooked a spanking-new housing development called Bell Fields. Plunked down in the middle of what was still mostly a sweep of cropland was a neat grid of what Tim called "phony Colon-ies," half-acre houses on one-acre lawns, houses with vinyl siding and each with two white colonnaded pillars holding up peaked porticoes— porches with light fixtures that Tim said cost more than the porches. Tim Brynn's parents and brother lived there, on one of those spiffy streets with names that the Chicago developers imagined would appeal to upstate New York sensibilities—names such as Pumpkin Hollow and Concord Green and Roanoke Way.

No one considered this place the "real" Ridgeline, although Tim envied his brother's sodded lawn, which was like the softest green suede (Tim's own lawn still occasionally sprouted alfalfa). But more of the in-towners were moving out to Bell Fields, where the walls might be thinner, but all the bathrooms had Jacuzzis. Gwenny liked the fact that her ranch had been a model and had been planted with at least six perennial gardens and a dozen fruit trees, to which she had added a dozen more gardens and six more fruit trees—until the facade itself was nearly completely concealed. Tim and his sister and brother said their parents' house resembled the kind of place anyone called Hansel or Gretel should avoid.

Campbell and Tim were in-town stalwarts. They held on, as did some older couples and some newlyweds—gentrifiers delighted at buying big old Gambrel houses for a song and then spending a hundred thousand dollars on new wiring and Jacuzzis.

Campbell was wearing her clingy little black dress and a red Irish cloak Tim had given her for her birthday.

"You look like a fallen woman," their father said. Campbell got all gooey and flirty.

Mallory wanted to gag.

When they got to Aunt Kate and Uncle Kevin's, Mally glanced around for new craft projects. This time, it was a snow village on the mantel—parent snow people and their three teeny round babies, made from Sculpey clay. Uncle Kevin and Aunt Kate's house never seemed to accumulate big drifts of magazines and clean laundry no one folded that was just moved from one corner to another when someone swept the floor. Even though they also had three kids, younger than the twins and Adam, their house always looked ready for the arrival of a photography crew from an interior-decorating magazine. Aunt Kate did all sorts of things Mallory liked, in theory, although she would have rather had an appendectomy with a dull stick than do them herself. Aunt Kate had baked a loaf of braided bread and shellacked it, then tied a gingham ribbon around it to match her blue kitchen curtains and table napkins.

Mallory didn't even know if her family *had* cloth table napkins. Her mom put a roll of paper towels in the middle of the table and told everyone to grab one at dinner—when she was home for dinner. When she wasn't, dinner was always what their father called "broccoli and something" that their mother had made earlier.

"Why don't you ever cook?" Mallory asked Tim. "Mom works. You work. She works as much as you work."

"Not really, because I own the store. There's a lot more . . . bill paying and stuff. We have a deal about cooking. She cooks and I . . . built the garage," Tim explained.

"You built the garage once, for six months, but she's been cooking for sixteen years," Mally said. "It's not really fair, is it?"

"I take you to Sunday school," Tim said.

"And sleep in the car."

"She works nights!" Tim said. "She works ten twelve-hour days and then has two straight weeks off! Come on! I only get three weeks a year off! Plus, you work at the store. I thought you were on my side."

"I was," Mallory said. "I guess I just didn't realize I used to be a sports feminist and not a real feminist."

"Heating *up* the broccoli and chicken is considered cooking," said Tim, in a last bid for his daughter's respect.

"Carrying in the bags is *not* considered shopping," Mally retorted.

For two weeks, Tim walked around pouting.

Then, in an elaborate gesture, he took a six-week cooking class at Hickory Woods Tech. The girls and Adam then got pasta and broccoli, pasta and shrimp, pasta and chopped tomatoes, pasta and ham, pasta *quattro formaggi*. Merry and Adam were mad at Mallory for complaining. They felt their gorges rise when they saw the blue boxes come out of the cupboard.

Mally was sorry she'd ever brought it up.

Maybe, Mally thought now, it was because Aunt Kate didn't work at all that she always seemed so calm.

Campbell was always pulling her hair up into spikes because

she was always late. She was always wondering aloud if a person could do CPR on herself.

Maybe Aunt Kate's house was the house of a person who didn't have stress. Uncle Kevin was a lawyer. Even the little girl cousins wore clothes from an English designer. Still, Mallory was proud of her mother. She couldn't imagine a life that had enough time for actually making fossilized bread. Campbell's job was boring, sticking needles into sad babies and old people so they didn't starve or dry up (Mallory had never seen Campbell in the exciting pressure cooker of the operating room). But it was a real *job*.

Merry completely disagreed.

She worshipped Aunt Kate's house.

She insisted that raising a family was a real job, too. Meredith wanted to have a dozen babies and make needlepoint pillows.

Mallory still wanted to grow up and one day be her dad's partner in the sporting goods store he owned with Rick Domini. She wished the store were called Brynn and Daughter, instead of Domino Sports. She loved working at the store on Saturdays, smelling the new ski gloves and leather boots, getting free basketballs and occasionally meeting very young (or very former) pro athletes who seemed to have gotten lost on the way to somewhere else at Domino Sports in Ridgeline.

But it wasn't really the shellacked bread that was so irritating tonight, Mally admitted to herself. Did she wish she were somewhere else tonight? Only with her entire soul. Even Mally, who was antisocial, wanted to be at a party tonight. People who babysat on New Year's Eve were considered the crud at the bottom of the social barrel, below girl computer geniuses (Mallory actually *was* sort of a girl computer genius).

But then, they hadn't even opened half their gifts yet. They'd decided to wait until tomorrow to make the delicious memory last longer. It had been a fabulous party.

And, to be honest, their parents really never did anything fancy, like Kate and Kevin did, such as dinner parties and Broadway shows. All they did was have Drew's parents and Bonnie and their brothers and sisters over to play board games.

In the summer, they all went for ten days to the family camp, and Tim and Campbell would drink beer and do wacky eighties dancing around the fire pit. When they went to movies, it was at the art cinema, for two dollars a ticket, to see old movies like *Lawrence of Arabia*—which they also forced on the twins.

Okay, they deserved their big night. But the twins both thought Campbell was overdoing the concerned-parent bit.

"We've just never left you alone and gone so far away before," Campbell went on.

And on and on.

Even Meredith finally gently reminded her mom, "We're hardly going to be alone. Grandma Gwenny will be here in a couple of hours."

Tim's mom was coming to sleep over with the children, no later than ten that night. Since Tim's father had a mild heart condition, they avoided large crowds and unfamiliar germs, and were having only a few friends over for bridge and a late supper. Tim's sister, Karin, who also lived in Deptford and was home because she, just like Campbell thirteen years before, was in the final stages of her pregnancy, was also on alert.

Nothing could go wrong.

"Stop worrying!" Mallory scolded her mother. "You know you just want to leave, so leave!"

"Mally," Meredith said. "Come on. You'd worry. There're a lot of kids here."

"But we have every number, in our pockets, up on the chalk-board, and next to the phone, for everybody from the pizza guy practically to the FBI!" Mallory protested.

She glanced at her little brother, Adam, with a grimace.

There was trouble on two legs. Adam had a gift.

He was deep in whispered conversation with his cousin, Alex, a year younger, and Mally knew something was up. Nearly eleven, Adam was a devious little creature. Maybe he *had* convinced Kim Jellico's brother, David, to give him fireworks. She knew Adam had asked. Kim had told them. And Mally had seen David just the morning before. He was cruising past the forest road near their house where Mally took her run. He didn't seem to be going anywhere and it was break, so why wasn't he asleep like a normal guy? Almost out of breath, Mally yelled out a warning to him: No way was he to give Adam fireworks! David just laughed.

"I'd never give fireworks to a little kid, even a little kid like you," he said. But David *was* a guy and prone to idiot jokes.

Mallory would never forget him popping up at Kim's bedroom window with a black nylon stocking over his face the night of Kim's eleventh birthday sleepover. The girls all screamed, and

Kirsten Morgan went hysterical (although Kirsten Morgan was always going hysterical).

Mally was the only one who didn't scream. She went outside and got up in David's face, yelling at him that he was a freako idiot. David wasn't even with his friends. He was alone and he was fourteen, old enough to know better. Merry called Mallory a jerk for yelling at David on Kim's birthday. But Merry would have forgiven David if he'd thrown a small hand grenade into the open window. She said boys were just immature.

She always got limp around David, looking at him from under her eyelashes. Like he would notice Merry in ten million years!

What if Adam had fireworks all strung together under the front porch right now? Adam *did* stay over with Alex the night of the party, only two days ago.

"Let's play hide-and-seek outside!" Mally announced as soon as all the parents were disposed of. Her little cousins Hannah and Heather, who were five and four, clapped their hands and ran for their coats.

"We're too big for hide-and-seek," Adam announced with elaborate apathy.

"You're too scared you can't beat me," Mally teased him. "You'll never be able to run as fast as I do. I'm an athlete!"

"Can so," Adam said.

"Can not," Mally answered. "The tree is goal and I'll give you to a hundred. Hannah, go back and get your boots on. It's freezing out here. One game!"

Once she was finally (supposedly) counting, Mallory got down on her hands and knees and crept a few feet under the porch. There was what appeared to be the world's largest collection of cracked old Frisbees under there, and a bike pump, and a feral cat that winked at her and disappeared, but nothing that looked like rockets or bombs. Behind her, she heard Adam shriek gleefully, "Home free!"

They played eight or nine games, using up more than an hour. Then they played flashlight tag for another half hour.

That ended when Hannah got lost in the neighbor's grape arbor—two acres over, as there were only two houses on the long road.

To placate Hannah, who was whining big time, Meredith made hot chocolate and Mallory set up a DVD on the life cycle of a lion cub for the little girls. Alex and Adam went up to Alex's room to play Mally's skater and soccer video games—as well as the Doom Slayers game her mother didn't know about. Mally didn't dare tell on Adam, who would tell on her right back. *That* had been the big whispering secret with Alex. Well, her mother hadn't asked her, point-blank, "Mallory, do you own an exceptionally violent computer game?" Had she? And so, strictly speaking, Mallory wasn't lying.

An hour later, the little cousins began to nag to put their party hats on.

"It's a little early," Merry told them. It was barely eight o'clock. "Let's eat first." She'd made the little kids macaroni and cheese with hot dogs sliced into it.

All the kids ate dutifully and put their dishes in the dishwasher.

Aunt Kate even had a magnet on it that read CLEAN ME or I'M CLEAN that she turned over when she started a new load.

Then Hannah asked, "Can we bang pans outside? Mom always lets us." The last sentence was a dead giveaway that this was a total lie.

"I don't know," Meredith said slyly. "Do you think you're old enough?"

"I do. I'm not afraid of the dark!" Hannah said stoutly, even though she'd been crying loud enough for people in Manhattan to hear her just an hour earlier.

"Well, then, let's see what we can find!"

"Aunt Kate probably doesn't want people banging on her French cookware!" Mally said with a hint of vinegar in her voice.

"Mal, don't be a butt pain."

"Well, she probably doesn't. . . ."

"Just take it easy." Meredith got out four of Aunt Kate's forty-five or so saucepans. She pulled out a big boiler and a frying pan and another wooden spoon when Alex suddenly confessed that he'd like to bang in the New Year as well. "What about you, Adam Ant?"

Adam simply sneered.

"Not everything fun is babyish," Merry told her brother. "And not everything babyish is bad."

They flipped on a news channel that promised festivities from around the world: There was already a rap group so new that even the twins didn't recognize them dancing around a big stage criss-crossed with racing lights.

Mallory would remember that she felt something not new, but unaccustomed as a conscious thought, in those final minutes.

She felt an intense and magnetic upsurge of love toward Merry. She smiled at her twin's funny, pretend-adult domestic ways—wiping up every drop of the children's dribbled chocolate from their hands, scooting Hannah and Heather into their footie pajamas and setting their parkas nearby, so that they could rush outside to bang on the pans and then be whisked into bed. To Mally, who lay on the couch the whole time, all this seemed impossibly dear. It was as if Mally was seeing Merry the way Merry would look when she was grown and a mother. But under the tide of affection was a kind of dismay—as if she, Mallory, might not actually be there with her twin when Merry was grown up.

She realized that she never thought of Meredith in terms of "love." Love was what she felt for family, best friends, even Kim's adorable dog, Tofu, or a song, a sport, a season like summer. How could she love Meredith? How could she love the sharp point of her own chin, the sound of her own voice spoken the way other people said they heard their own voices on a recording? She *was* Meredith.

"Giggy," she said to Mally, who looked up with a full-blown smile. It was one of the oldest of their twin words, and neither had any idea what it had once meant. Perhaps it simply meant love.

"Happy birthday, Ster," Mally said. Adam jumped up and took the cue, pulling from each pocket a plastic bag tied with a ribbon. He handed one to each of the girls. Inside was a charm: a megaphone for Merry, a soccer ball for Mally.

"You can pin them on your sweater with diaper pins, like Kim," he said. "Happy birthday, Ster." There was a moment of quiet among the three of them before Mallory reached out and gave Adam's hair a soft tug.

The charms would later be found in the yard, under a frosting of broken glass.

They hauled Adam across both their laps and started tickle-torturing him in gratitude.

Then all three were all but knocked backward by a sudden uprush of air from the half-open double doors at the front of the house.

The plastic covering Uncle Kevin had put in place of the screen flew off with a whickering sound.

And then, the very windows shook in their frames with the force of the explosion.

"What the hell is that?" Merry shouted.

All of them could see vivid angry outbursts rocketing up from every window. They heard the whistle and saw fountains of red, gold, green. Next came the staccato of strings of firecrackers and the deep gutturals of cherry bombs.

"Cool!" Adam shouted, over the screams of the younger children. "Is this why you were going on about the fireworks? Is it a surprise?"

"Adam Brynn!" Mallory shouted, noticing that Hannah and Heather were now crying hard and clinging to Merry. "Look at how much you scared the little kids. I told you, no fireworks!"

Adam's freckled face was a map of shocked betrayal. "Me? Those aren't mine! I don't know what they are!"

All six of them ran out the front door, but the girls couldn't focus: Fireworks were exploding behind the house, too, in the rock garden, near the back door.

"I don't see anybody!" Mally yelled.

"Me neither!" said Merry, trying to keep both Hannah and Heather from simultaneously climbing her like a jungle gym. The fireworks weren't corner-store sparklers, but big, deafening, semi-pro, the real thing.

"Should we call the fire department?" Merry asked over the din.

"They don't seem to be doing anything, just exploding," Mallory shouted as they herded the kids back onto the porch. "Adam, swear on Mom's head, you didn't know a thing about this?"

"I swear. I asked David Jellico to get fireworks for me ten times, and he wouldn't!"

Merry's cell phone began to vibrate in her hip pocket and to play "Song of Joy." She answered: It was Will Brent, wishing her a happy birthday.

"I can't talk," she said. "Some neighborhood idiot set off a mess of fireworks, and it's not even midnight!" She glanced up at Mallory. "Me too," she said quietly. Mallory smirked. Then the telephone inside the house began to ring and they ran for it. By the time the twins got everyone back inside and explained to their grandmother that what she was hearing through the receiver was not a gunfight on Pumpkin Hollow Road, they were too exhausted to do anything but flop down into the big couch under the front window.

Merry thought of it first.

Why had Gwenny called?

It wasn't near time for her to come over.

"What's up, Grandma?" she remembered asking.

"I was thinking about those fireworks," Grandma Gwenny had said.

But no one had told Grandma Gwenny about the fireworks until after she called.

She could be as strange as they were.

"Don't worry," Grandma had said. "It was just a prank. No one is hurt. Right? You're sure? I'll be there soon."

"No one is hurt. But you sound funny. What's wrong?"

"Nothing," Gwenny Brynn said. And she told herself, *Be still, Gwen, it's nothing!* But she knew it was *something* . . . though not what the something was.

"What was all that about?" Meredith asked. "Did you arrange with Grandma to call?"

"Not me," Mally said.

"So what do you think that was? Who did it? The neighbors?"

"I don't even think the neighbors are over there. Their house is totally dark."

"Maybe they were inside making out."

"And then they jumped up from making out and decided to set off eighty million fireworks all around the house of the people next door?"

"There is that," Merry admitted.

"It was probably Will," Mallory ventured, knowing even as she said it that Will Brent was as likely to pull off a scary practical joke as the girl at the Video Box was likely to be polite.

"You know it wasn't."

"Well, he called right then!"

"He knew it was the time I was putting the little kids to bed. Well, almost time. He's at Lizzy White's party. He knew it was a time when I could talk. I should call him back."

"Do you have to? Right now?"

"No," Merry said finally. "He can wait. You're supposed to let guys wait."

Mally asked, "Are you hungry?"

"Only so I could eat my own leg. Maybe Grandma will bring something. She'll be here any minute, trust me. She sounded all weird. She probably thinks we're dead out in the yard," Merry answered.

"She'll bring cucumber and cream cheese on toast squares!" Mallory said with a laugh.

"I can't wait!" Merry yelled. "I just love those cucumber sandwiches. You only have to eat fifty!"

The girls exchanged grins.

"Let's make toasted bagels and tomatoes with cheese," they said together.

"I'll make," Merry offered. "I think they're finally asleep." Adam was sprawled, of all places, on the dog's bed in the corner of the living room.

"Me too," Mallory said. "I'm so totally excited by babysitting and idiot fireworks I could party all night. But I think I'll get a ten-minute power nap instead."

"You'll sleep through your own funeral," Merry said, echoing their father in his litany of complaints about Mallory's comatose Saturday mornings.

"God, I hope so," Mallory said.

She lay back on the sofa.

She was drowsy, almost asleep, when the roof fell in. A five-foot burning column from the porch crashed through the roof just over Mallory's head.

Before Merry could cross the room, their aunt's huge brocaded curtains caught and disintegrated, with a sound like a million crushed pine needles, into huge golden torches that fell like fronds onto the couch. Mallory clawed to keep the strands, pliant and sticky as hot sugar, away from her face.

"Get on the floor! Roll!" Merry screamed as Mallory leaped up, the back of her sweater alight. Merry pushed her sister down and, once sure that Mallory had rolled out the flames and ripped the sweater off as well, leaped up the stairs two at a time. She dragged Hannah and Heather from their bunks and forced them down into a four-legged crawl toward the back stairs, shouting for Alex, who appeared, groggy, in his basketball pajamas, at the door of his room.

"The house is on fire!" Merry shouted. "The porch roof is on fire! It broke the front window!"

Smoke was filling the hall. Merry couldn't figure it out. Somehow, the flames must have penetrated the roof. Glancing into her aunt's room, she noticed the three baby albums prominently displayed on a whitewashed bookshelf. Ever tenderhearted, Merry dashed to grab them. But as she did, little Heather screamed and scooted under her mother's bed.

"Alex!" Meredith shouted. "Get Hannah downstairs. Get Adam outside. See if Mally's hurt!" His eyes huge, Alex stood still in his doorway, staring. Smoke was beginning to curl around the molding, and the smoke alarms were shrieking. Merry's throat began to sting. "Alex, go!"

Alex seemed to find his feet and began to run. Merry couldn't believe how fast all of it was happening. Coughing, she threw the baby albums down the stairs and crawled across her aunt and uncle's floor. "Heather! Heather Lynn! Come out here!" She could see Heather, back against the wall under her parents' headboard. But small as she was, Merry couldn't work her way under the bed. Heather had thrown herself on her face and was sobbing for her mother. The smoke was thickening. Merry could hear a rumpus downstairs—Mally screaming Adam's name, the other two crying, the door banging open. Finally, with a mighty lunge that opened a gash in her scalp when she hit her head on the bed frame, Meredith grabbed Heather's long braid and pulled the squirming child toward her.

Meredith picked Heather up and held her like a football, as the child fought and choked. Merry tripped over the photo albums on the landing and fell down three steps. Grabbing them, she scrabbled for the back door, pushing Heather ahead of her with her knee. A full second passed before the message reached Merry's brain that the doorknob was oven-hot and the skin on her hand was already bubbling. She screamed, instinctively turning toward the sink. But the kitchen curtains were crackling. Meredith couldn't even see into the living room.

"Mallory!" Meredith called. "Mally!"

Mallory didn't reply.

In the fractional instant it took her to realize that Mallory might not answer, that she might not hear Mally's voice again except inside her head, Meredith experienced the same yearning her twin had felt hours before.

Giggy, she thought. Without Mallory, she would not feel halved but erased. She would need to draw herself again from a stick figure, filling in her shape and textures. She would be a flat Meredith, who would disappear when she turned in profile, a silhouette Meredith without color or sound.

"Mallory!" Even to herself, she sounded like a wounded lamb, bleating.

She thought she heard a faint answer—where did it come from? The billowing blackness of the living room, the ring of flame left by the open front door? When had all the electricity gone out?

"Mallory!" Merry called again.

Quickly she pushed Heather out the back door—nothing out back was burning now. Merry watched to make sure that Heather jumped down the steps and ran into the yard. Then she grabbed one of the little girl's coats from the rack and covered her mouth. She dropped to her knees and began to crawl on her elbows toward what she thought should be the couch under the bay window. When she felt what seemed to be Mallory's shoulder, she hauled her sister on top of her and began to scoot backward toward the door, inch by laborious inch. She could see a lighter rectangle of darkness. *Finally.* Then she heard a pop and shivering musical sounds of tinkling glass, and then nothing else at all.

FOREVER TWO

They lay in a dream, but the dream wasn't like sleep. It was like suffocation.

Neither knew how long it lasted.

Both of them were less troubled by the pain than the unnatural sensation of being unable to hear each other, except dully, as if through a blanket. But time indeed was measured by painful interruptions—the positioning of needles, the reflexive gagging on tubes. Their own groans sounded distant, as if their bodies and voices were a radio left on in an empty room. One sister's thoughts were indistinct to the other, expanding and contracting in shapes rather than in words. They caught mental glimpses: Difficult, congested breathing for Mallory. Merry's heartbeat taking off at the approach of a claw that would pull and pinch off skin that was as parched as a dead leaf.

After a time, the sense of morning, the change of light, even behind closed eyelids, returned.

That came first.

Next they heard the oceanic murmur of voices that would rise and subside. Thousands of dots collected into pictures, and faces appeared. Between the girls the images ping-ponged—tiny and far off, or close and stretched, grotesque, misshapen, and huge. First to Merry, then to Mally, there appeared snapshots, for a single second. They saw their father, asleep in a chair. They saw their grandmother Arness, Campbell's mother, on her farmhouse porch in Virginia. But Grandma Arness was dead. She died when they were ten. They saw Grandma Gwenny peering at them, her wild Welsh eyes, so like their own, filled with aching empathy. Nodding, nodding. Grandma Gwenny cried and nodded. There was Gramps outside Uncle Kevin's house, clutching his cell phone, his face streaked red and gray by the fire and shadow. Their mother, bending low, brushing their cheeks, flooding them with their mother's smell—gardenia and rubbing alcohol. The sting of her tears on Mally's face. Adam, his mouth opening in a dark, sucking, expanding cry.

The night images were worse.

First Merry, then Mally, cringed when a tiny black-haired girl in an old-fashioned high-necked dress appeared, leaning over a bridge above a creek, then turned quickly to stare at them, her face zooming nearer, nearer, nearer—her eyes nearly flat against their own eyes. Meredith and Mallory clutched at each other's minds in fear. The little girl's face was kind and even familiar, but overflowing with knowledge and mourning. Then David Jellico, in a garden, carefully arranging great circles of smooth white stones or shells. Merry thought it was a religious place. Mally thought it was a graveyard.

They ran away into sleep.

Finally real people appeared.

Kim came, sobbing, pleading with Merry to wake up, kissing Merry when she opened her eyes and blinked to show that she was already awake. Will Brent knelt at Merry's bedside in prayer.

Mally, still in and out of consciousness, saw her teammates, led by her friend Eden, carrying a signed ball through the hospital's revolving door. And then they appeared in her room, for real.

"Way to get attention, Brynn," Eden said. "Don't expect to get out of practice this way." Except it sounded like *donexpectogeddoudda* . . .

Finally, each heard words distinct as musical notes: The voice of Dr. Staats, their pediatrician. Their father's. "Undeniable." "Without them . . ." "Permanent . . ." "Breathing, at first . . ."

Mallory wrenched her mind up and out.

She opened her eyes. What lay over her? A tent? A plastic sheet? In her nose . . . in her nose was a plastic tube. She tugged lightly on it and choked.

She tried to think her way to Meredith, but she heard only a mewling, like a kitten. Meredith was deep under some kind of syrupy layering, a mental mud of medication. Only when someone changed the dressings on her hand did Meredith stir from the fog of painkillers. As she watched dimly, the nurses replacing the dressings, she would think of her hand as it had been—fluttering, pointing, directing, thrust up in the Y sign, snapping back

and forth across her green cheerleader's sweater in the gestures
of the routines, waving when she flirted with the crowd on the
bleachers, calling out instructions under her breath to the rest of
the squad, "Last time now . . . Ridgeline, so fine!"

No, she thought.

And, for the first time, Mally heard her clearly. That one word.
In separate rooms, both girls struggled to sit up.

"Hey! Hey! Hi there!" Tim said, jumping out of his chair when
he saw Mallory strain against her pillows. "Thank God, oh thank
God. Hold on! Go slow, honey."

More gently than he had ever held his rough-and-tumble child,
Tim Brynn slid an arm under Mallory's back and asked, "Are you
awake awake now, Mal? Mallory? Do you understand what I'm
saying? You gave us quite a scare, little one. You've been out of it,
well, in and out of it, since the fire. Three *days* ago, Mally. You're a
hero, you know? Did you know that? Alex and Adam and the little
girls would never have made it without you two. Don't. Don't try
to talk. You sucked in half a houseful of smoke." When she pointed
to her face, Tim said, "That's oxygen going in through your nose,
and purified air around you. Your face was just scorched, like a
bad sunburn. No scars. I promise." Ill at ease, when he ought to be
happy, for a reason he didn't quite understand, Tim hurried on,
sharing with Mallory a list of details that might have been important to her at any other time but this. "Actually, it's amazing that
the house is not that bad. They're staying with us now, but the
worst thing was the smoke damage. And the porch is wrecked, of
course." He added, "You'll be out in a few days. I should ring for
the nurse. . . ."

Why isn't he telling me? Mallory wondered. *He knows it's the first thing I would want to hear.*

On the other side of the wall, Campbell said to Meredith, "Please, honey, stop trying to talk. The oxygen tube isn't going to let you, anyhow. Your chest is going to hurt for a while, not to mention your poor little hand. And you'll probably have the worst sore throat ever. Are the pain meds helping?"

Meredith writhed on the bed. *How do they expect me to rest when I can't hear her? I'm not sure if she can hear me or if I'm dreaming. Why don't they know?*

Campbell said, "Merry-heart. I'll never forgive . . . myself. I shouldn't have gone. It was so selfish. . . ." Meredith waved that away, gently shaking her head and pointing at her nose. Campbell recognized the ancient gesture that, in the family, meant *"pay attention!"* Merry looked hard at her mother, unblinking, and touched her heart. Misunderstanding, Campbell broke into tears and said, "I love you, too." Meredith tapped her heart again, more urgently. Beneath the huge mitt of her bandages, she felt the reprimand of the pain.

She turned her head away from Campbell.

In her own room, Mallory lay back, exhausted and frustrated.

Tim went on, "Honey, don't get upset. You're going to be good as new. . . ." Struggling, Mally pointed at her head. Tim tried to interpret what she was saying "Think? How did it happen?" Mally put up two fingers, pointed to her right hand, and shrugged elaborately. *Right-handed*, she tried to tell her father, *right-handed*. She was so used to communicating without so much effort! "Honey, it wasn't the fireworks. We don't know who set off the fireworks.

Maybe it was the same person who set the fire, maybe it was someone different. What I mean is, it was set in a different way. Some kid threw a gasoline bomb, or whatever, on the roof—gasoline in a Coke bottle for all we know. There was glass up there. God only knows why. Kevin never met a stranger in his life."

In the next room, Merry gathered her strength and her bandaged paw, then pointed to her left hand. *Left-handed, Mom*, she tried to tell Campbell. *Left-handed*. She had to know, and before she got too sleepy.

In answer, her mother said, "They don't know who did it. It blew up. They assume a car full of drunk kids . . ."

Meredith croaked.

"Don't talk," Campbell soothed her. "Shush now."

"Mally . . ."

"I'm sorry. I just assumed you two . . . you know. Could hear, like always. Your sister is fine. She inhaled smoke, but she'll be fine," Campbell assured her. Campbell wanted to kick herself. More than Tim did, she understood about the tin-can telephone that joined her daughters. "You saved her life, darling. You pulled her out onto the back porch." Campbell began to cry, fresh unchoked rivulets of tears.

Next door, Mallory first tapped, then pounded on her chest.

Tim nodded and said, "Yes, you inhaled smoke." Mally made her eyes go wide and shook her head violently. Tim reached under the clear tent and gently held Mallory's shoulders down against the sheets. "Look, Mallory. You need to be quiet now, honey." Mallory pounded her small chest more frantically. "What?" Tim asked.

"Don't get hysterical . . . I'll get paper." He gave Mallory a pencil and a sheet ripped from the telephone book. Mally began to write. Tim ran for Campbell.

"Oh, my baby!" Campbell cried, diving, oblivious of the protocols, into the tent. "We were so scared you wouldn't wake up. Merry was sedated, but you . . . you just wouldn't wake up!" Campbell's face was smeared with cold tears and spent mascara. She turned to her husband. "You did tell her that Meredith is okay? I don't think they can hear each other."

"What?" Tim asked. "Hear each other? They can't even talk, Cam."

Campbell ignored him.

"You know Merry is okay, don't you?" Campbell asked Mallory. Mallory shook her head.

Tim put his hand over his eyes.

"Your sister is fine," he said. "That's what she meant, pounding on her chest. Me. She was saying 'me.' She meant 'my twin.'" *Finally*. Dad was great, but so thick sometimes.

"Meredith pulled you out of the fire," Campbell said. "You were this close to the burning couch, and the couch and curtains were an inferno. She . . . does have a bad burn on one of her palms." Mallory cringed. "But she'll heal. It's not nearly as bad as it could have been."

Mallory fell back, spent, and despite the flicker of guilt, was soon asleep. The paper she had clasped in her hand slipped to the floor. When a nurse picked it up later, she could barely make out the scrawled words: *Merry, Merry, Merry.*

HEROES AND VILLAINS

HEROES AND VILLAINS

B y the end of their first week back at school, Mallory was sick and tired of everyone treating them like little china dolls. It was January, and still no snow, only bleak sleet and mud.

Everybody was so bored that all they could talk about was the fire.

And when they talked about the fire, Mally felt like an idiot.

Mally's temper matched the weather.

Her voice was no longer hoarse. She still felt dizzy when she ran and had to stop over and over. Both girls had chest X-rays and a frightening examination of their lungs called a broncho-scope that showed, remarkably, nothing much. Despite all that they might have inhaled—from soot to charred fibers. Mallory possibly because she lay facedown, Merry because she held the coat over her face—their lungs seemed relatively fine and would soon be normal.

Despite the physical healing, Mally somehow didn't feel whole . . . or like herself. If she could not undo the past and will the fire never to have happened, she wished at least that people would stop *talking* about it.

There was the big burst of attention just afterward.

"Don't you hate this?" Mallory asked Merry one night. Someone from Canada called to ask if they'd be on the radio, and before Merry could stop her, Mally told the woman, "We're not allowed."

"No, actually, I think it's great," Merry said. "Why shouldn't we get credit? We, like, almost died. We saved the kids."

"You're supposed to save your brother and your cousins, duh," Mally said. "If we were, like, pioneers, our parents would have already forgotten this. Kids our age pulled their brothers and sisters out of burning tents and junk all the time."

"Well, we're not like pioneers." Merry was sleeping with an eye mask these days, in case someone wanted to take her picture in the morning.

"I just want it to end."

"I just want it to last forever," Merry insisted. "My whole season is ruined. I might as well have some fun." Her picture was being zipped around the county by every kid with a cell phone in Ridgeline. The knowledge of her real, if fleeting, fame was a cozy little cushion of contentment inside her.

Mallory wished she could be invisible.

For starters, in the newspaper photo taken just after they left the hospital, Mally thought that her face, although barely swollen anymore, looked like a ripe plum. She was annoyed every time she had to thank someone for giving her a copy of the picture—as if she might have missed it! She had enough to fill two photo albums!

The headline read, TWINS SAVE SIBS IN BIRTHDAY BLAZE. Pictured with them were the editor of the *Ridgeline Reporter*, Fred Elliott, as well as the mayor, Joan Karls, and Wendell von Pelling, the fire chief. Chief von Pelling looked sheepish, as well he might. The first two calls about a fire were thought to be hoaxes because they obviously came from teenagers, with laughter and the sounds of loud music in the background. The department responded, but there was grumbling. When Grandpa Brynn called, he gave the dispatcher a piece of his mind along with a description of the disaster and reminded her that his son was a lawyer and might sue the department.

The officials presented each of the twins with Public Service medals and five-hundred-dollar scholarships from the state Police and Fire Association.

Much sweeter were the little notes from Hannah and Heather and Alex. Hannah's began, "We love Twin . . ." (Their cousins, like most of their teachers, couldn't tell Mallory and Meredith apart, and called them, separately and collectively, "Twin.") Aunt Kate was ridiculously moved by Meredith's gutsy effort to save the baby books. She bought her a hundred-dollar gift certificate to Scrips-and-Scraps—which Merry intended to use entirely for commemorating her cheerleading career. For Mallory, her aunt and uncle provided a year's worth of weekly tickets to the Overture Cinema Center in Deptford. Mally was grateful, but didn't know how her aunt thought she was going to pop over to the

Deptford Mall on her own. Maybe Drew or Eden would take her.

Drew came over every day to look at her like she was a science project. "I can't believe you went through that," he said, and begged for detail after detail. He brought Mally two more of his outgrown cross-country shirts and one that was new. "All guys are pyros," Drew said. "But this had to be some kind of psycho if he knew people were in there."

"Maybe it was a girl," Mally suggested, just to bug him.

"No, a girl wouldn't do that. I looked it up."

"Oh, well, if you looked it up . . ." Mallory mocked him. Drew's face flushed. Mally felt sorry for redheads: They would never be able to play poker.

"It's true. Girls don't have the same thing with fire. They'll catch him, though, because they always make a mistake."

"The one who burned down the church in Tremont didn't."

"That's the one fire everyone always brings up. . . ." Drew said. "But I read about it on the Internet, and it said they always make a mistake. Like on purpose. They're proud of what they do. Arsonists. I don't know about that church in Tremont. Maybe somebody did it who's already in jail for something else. Whenever I talk about this, someone mentions the church."

"That's because it was the only other one there was," Mally told him. "We don't get a lot of arson in Ridgeline. I Googled the last murder. It was in 1956. That was, like, years before my mother was born."

"Who was it?" Drew asked.

"Guy shot his wife's boyfriend. Very boring."

"What about the cat murders?" he asked Mallory.

"I'm not counting cat murders. People poison cats all the time. It's creepy, but people just hate cats. There actually are too many cats, Drewsky. And cats don't really like people, either."

"I like my cat," Drew objected. His ancient one-eyed cat, Fluffy, slept every night practically on Drew's head. Drew smelled like shampoo and mint kitty litter.

"Do you want to go to the movies?" Mally finally asked.

Drew blushed again. "Like, with you?" he mumbled.

"No, like by yourself," Mally replied. "I'm not asking you out! God! That would only be so sick."

Drew personally didn't think it was sick. He adored Mallory and couldn't wait until she was fifteen, when Campbell and Tim would allow "group dates." He would come back from college for it. If he waited only forever, he knew Mallory would marry him. But Mally said, "It's just that my aunt gave me enough movie passes to last until I'm thirty for saving the kids."

"Well, you did."

"Yeah, but it wasn't like I had a choice. Merry did it all. I was out of it. . . ."

"Still, Mallory. People run from fires. I've heard of parents running from a fire with their own kids inside."

"No way."

"Way," Drew said.

"Did you Google that, too?"

"No," Drew said. He had.

Mallory sighed and said, "Well, I'm watching *Days* here, if you don't mind. So do you want to go to the movies? Or should I just give you some of the fourteen thousand passes I have and you can take a real girl?"

"I'll go," Drew told her. "You'll have to wear a mask, though."

Mallory threw her hands up over her face. Drew wanted to punch himself. She thought he meant the faint rosy remains of the scorch burns on her face.

"I only meant that everyone recognizes you."

"I'll go dressed as Meredith. I'll put on false eyelashes."

"That'll do it. No one will recognize Meredith," Drew said. "I feel better already."

Later that day, Drew hung around outside the dining room while Mallory and Meredith were interviewed by the state fire inspector. Mallory didn't tell Drew, but she found the state fire investigator sexy and fascinating, though he was old, probably thirty.

The girls sat side by side across from him at the dining room table. From his briefcase, he took a stack of photos and a folder filled with dozens of reports detailing anonymous tips. He used a fountain pen, like Mallory's father, and squared a clean stack of blank paper before he wrote down the date and *Third Brynn Twins Interview*.

"Now that you're home and all well, think about it. Did you see anyone? Did you hear anything?" he asked. "The least little thing, something you wouldn't think would matter, could be the key to all of it. Think hard." He studied their eyes, to prompt them and to search for the hint of a lie.

"Not one single thing," Merry said. "Not even one car went by that we saw."

"Everybody else saw cars. Why not you?"

"We were taking care of the little kids, not staring out the windows," Mally told him.

"There had to be a car. We saw tire marks, marks with mud in them. Someone pulled over and parked in front of your uncle's house. They were new tires, though. No special wear pattern. Could match almost any car."

Mallory loved the way he talked. She decided to try to talk in partial sentences herself.

Seemed normal. Could have been anyone. Possible stranger. No personal involvement. She liked the swagger of it.

In the end, nothing about the fire investigation gave up a scintilla of new information.

All they knew was that the fireworks had been placed in advance, and ignited easily—concealed by dry leaves with a barrier made of cardboard around them. They'd been lit by hand, probably with a cheap cigarette lighter, almost certainly by someone wearing work gloves. There were scorched fabric fibers that would have matched only every one of ten thousand or so pairs of gloves sold just in the week since Christmas.

Everybody in Ridgeline apparently had seen more cars drive up and down the dead-end cul-de-sac of Pumpkin Hollow Road than anyone had seen that night on the New Jersey Turnpike, judging from the number of phone tips. But not one had seen a single human being. No one had even seen the children playing outside the house! No one, even people just a block away, witnessed the fireworks. No one had seen an explosive device thrown onto the roof. Everyone was somewhere else. That was what the arsonist had counted on. Police figured the callers just wanted in on the excitement.

The neighbors next door had indeed been out, returning home at two a.m. to find, to their horror, their street clogged with fire trucks, firefighters, and squad cars from three villages. The only thing that turned up in the neighbors' yard was the burnt end of what might have been a long fuse.

From the scorch mark, it was apparent that something big had flamed out on the back porch, evidently intended to block that route of escape. It was all planned to do serious damage, and yet, not serious enough to insure that kind of damage. Something about it was amateurish, but deliberately or . . . because it was the work of an amateur? The fire inspector told the locals that it was almost like someone was trying to scare the girls *almost* to death rather than kill them outright. The pyrotechnics might have gone further than the perpetrator intended.

A prank that got out of hand, the officials finally figured. The only question was, why that house? The isolated location was the best guess. The girls were well known, but their school friends called them nice and popular. The twins had no enemies. In fact, Edensau Cardinal, a beautiful, dark-haired sophomore, told officers, "No one would hurt Mally and Merry. Twins are sacred."

And though the police officers thought the comment was about as nuts as everything else about this case, and warranted a long look into Eden's background, she was just as pure as the twins. An athlete, a good student from a big family, she spent most of her time taking care of younger siblings and cousins, working Sundays at the Sunglass Nook in Deptford. She didn't even date. The twins' uncle, Kevin Brynn, was a real-estate lawyer. No one was in jail because of his job. No one was even angry with him over a divorce.

No one in Ridgeline had a bad word to say about *any* of the Brynns.

At last, there was nothing left to ask, nothing left to tell, nothing.

The town as a whole seemed to make a summary decision to let the girls get on with their lives—at least, the adults did. The kids wouldn't have let go of this drama if they were paid to do it. Gossip about the fire still raced through the halls of the middle school and high school. At the Brynns' house, there was a constant parade of visitors—everyone standing in front of the TV as Mally tried to watch *Days* or *General Hospital*. The girls' bedroom was like a florist's shop. Music boxes, teddy bears, and earrings were brought, like offerings. For Merry, it was like a second Christmas or birthday—with the added drama of all her friends' complete and utter fascination.

Even David Jellico visited once (Mally noticed he had a sweater tied around his neck and one half of his shirt tucked into his pants, with the other end out in front in a show-off way). And though he seemed bored and waiting for a chance to escape the whole time, Meredith acted like there was a rock band in the living room and was annoyed when Mallory kept turning the volume up on the TV. Frankly, Meredith was worn out from having to change outfits for the arrival of different boys.

Will Brent and Dane Greenberg came.

"Someone is going to pay," Dane said.

"No one hurts the M and M and gets away with it," Will said.

Meredith loved this even more.

"It's like being the total girl of the school," she said. "Like being homecoming queen or something."

"It's like being a weenie," Mallory told her. "All you had to do to get so popular was almost burn up." Even Tim kept walking around, punching the air and swearing he was going to black somebody's eye. Like their father would ever punch anyone out. Please. Mallory got aggravated with being treated like a little dumpling someone had to protect.

Everyone was convinced that the villain was someone they knew.

Mally was convinced of that much, too. She had the unkind, creepy thought that David Jellico did it—not meaning to hurt anyone, but to scare her for standing up to him at Kim's party two years ago.

"I don't think he meant it to go that far, but he's an ass," she told Merry.

"You're the ass," Merry said. "That's so mean and stupid. Bonnie is Mom's best friend."

"So David can't be a wingnut. I see."

"He was at a party in Deptford with Deirdre Bradshaw," Merry said. "They got there at, like, nine. Deidre is so beautiful. I would have a hard time getting him away from her."

"Being in Deptford would still give him time, you twit!" Mally said.

"I think you're the one who really has a crush on him," said Merry. "Like he's going to say, 'Hey, I have to stop and set fire to Kevin Brynn's house before we go to the party'?"

Mally gave up.

They missed the first two weeks of the second semester, but all their teachers were so sympathetic, neither one had to make up a single thing. Most even gave them all the class notes. Boys fell all over Merry, carrying her book bag because of her injury. Merry felt like a medieval princess with champions vying for her hand.

Her hand.

The scars were getting better, but they were still a mess.

All the attention was small compensation for missing her whole basketball cheering season, but still. Every week, the bandages were smaller. Every week, there was more healthy tissue that her mother carefully treated with antibiotics and gels. But she still couldn't hold a pencil. Her teachers wrote down all her answers for her.

Well.

At least the lower half of her body was undamaged.

Merry was too optimistic to sink down into a full depression. She stayed in focus on being ready for competition in March. She sat on the sidelines, a peppy little hero with her hand matching the white of the sweaters they wore with the big green letter *R* on the front. She spent early mornings in the gym, working her legs on the curling machine, practicing endless but careful combinations of jumps and splits and stretches—anything that didn't involve her hands. She could practice arm movements and choreography to music with the squad, but no one dared throw her on a mount or even let her balance on the hand of the one boy on the team, Kellen Fish, although she'd been practicing partner stunting in private, years before she technically should have done it. Merry's combination of balance and strength was so tempting that Coach Everson allowed it, but only reluctantly.

"You should be in college for this," she said every time Merry threw herself into a handspring and Kellen caught her and elevated her into a Statue of Liberty.

But anything extreme was out of the question now. Coach laid down the law.

Caitlin Andersen had taken over as the captain, and Kiley Karzniak as flyer. Merry was furious.

One night, Kim and Merry were lying on Kim's bed, sharing a pizza (Kim wouldn't eat the crusts and Merry wouldn't eat the middles, so it worked out well). The windows were open because the weather was so warm, but they had called everyone they knew and there wasn't a single thing to do. Crystal's house had been TP'ed and Wade Greenberg had already been grounded for it, and it was only nine o'clock.

"I want to tell you something," Kim said.

"Okay," Merry answered.

"It's kind of deep."

"That's okay."

"It's like, you did this good thing, and you get only bad things," Kim said. "It's like being cursed. Not really. But kind of."

"I got a lot of good things," Merry said. "I mean, I saved my brother's life. You don't get to feel much better than that." But she didn't sound convinced. "Of course, like Mallory says, I would have saved Adam anyway. It's not like it was anything special. If we were pioneers, we'd have had to pull him out of a flood a couple of times by now, probably."

"Why do you say that?"

"Mallory did. She thinks it's sick that everybody made such a big deal out of us doing stuff we were supposed to do anyhow."

"But your life is totally messed up!" Kim said, her eyes glistening with unspent tears.

"Well, thanks," said Merry.

"I didn't mean it that way," Kim apologized. "I meant messed up for now! I just feel so bad for you. You're like somebody on the Lifetime Channel."

David appeared in the hall, dressed in his brown leather jacket—Merry loved that it was *brown* leather, not black like some hoodlum or white like a gangster. He looked to her like old pictures of Charles Lindbergh in her history book, thin and straight and tall, like a Norse god with his brown eyes and blond hair. Did Italians have blond hair? Was David adopted? No, Campbell said that Bonnie got pregnant with David just a year after they began working together on the surgical floor at the hospital. David was just . . . gifted, where looks were concerned. Kim was cute, but not like her brother. Under the leather jacket, David wore one of those white sweaters that felt oily when you touched it. Merry wished she could.

"You don't look Italian," Merry said, curling her knees under her butt in a kitten's pose, hoping to prolong the moment.

"*Como!*" David explained. "*Tutti* blonds in the Alps."

"You speak Italian?"

"He's *taking* it," Kim put in. "There's a distance course for Latin and Italian and Japanese. Our dad speaks a little. Our one grandpa hardly spoke any English."

"It comes naturally," David said. "*Va bene! Multo grazie!*"

"Pizza! Gorgonzola!" Kim mocked him. "That's such crap. I hear you repeating the sentences until one in the morning!"

"It's the language of love. And what you don't know is that I'm dictating my novel!"

"David!" Meredith exclaimed. "Are you really a writer, too?"

"What do you mean, 'too'?" Kim asked. "What else does he do, golf? He's not dictating a novel. He talks to himself! He answers! He's done it all his life!"

"Shut up, fat butt! I want to be able to sound halfway educated when I go to college. Unlike some people. And as for golf, Tiger Woods will be a billionaire if he isn't already. At least it's a real sport!" David abruptly jumped into the air, landed in a spread-eagle stance with one arm thrust in front and one above his head, and cried, "Ridgeline, so fine! Rah-rah, team! They're all even lousy teams!"

Kim threw her apple core at David's head and nailed him.

"Hah!" she cried, but not before David could whip it back, and hard. It left a red mark. *Brothers*, Merry thought, but Kim looked puzzled and hurt. David headed out, for a date with Deirdre, Meredith assumed. That night, when she and Kim finally fell asleep, she dreamed again of David arranging stones in a garden. He looked so serious and sweet, his hair curling with the raindrops. He was a gentle boy, who must love flowers. Or it was his and Bonnie's vegetable garden. She wanted to marry a boy who loved his mother.

The next morning, she asked Kim, "Where does David work? Does he have a garden? You don't have a rock garden at your grandparents' house, do you?"

"No!" Kim said. "What do you mean?"

"Like big circles of stones or shells?"

"Oh, he'd kill you!" Kim said. She fell back into her ten orange polka-dotted feather pillows, laughing.

"What?"

"Did you follow him?"

"No."

"Did he tell you?"

"Kind of."

"Well, David acts like he's all that, but he's totally a baby when it comes to animals and stuff. He used to bring home these cats that had been abused or were just hopelessly sick. If they lived, he gave them to the vet to find homes for them, but if they died, he buried them . . . well, not far from your family camp. This has been since we were little kids. My mom used to drive him there.

He even had funerals for the hamsters. He used to say they liked being on the mountain."

"That's so sweet."

"Don't talk about it with him, though," Kim said. "I'm surprised he mentioned it. It's not this big macho thing to do. He even puts flowers up there."

Merry wished she could be just two years older, no matter what her mother always warned about wishing her life away. Having a guy who was that sensitive, and cute, and . . . David was like a song or something, except human.

That morning as she was eating breakfast, she said to David, "I won't tell anyone."

"What?"

"About the pets and the little graves. It's so sweet."

"What? What are you talking about?" David asked, his face changed, hardened.

"Forget I said anything," Merry said. It was clearly a tender spot.

"Really? What are you talking about?"

"About the cats you tried to rescue, that died . . . Kim told me . . . I think it's really—"

"Kim's fricking crazy! I did that when I was, like . . . ten. Kim's out of her mind." Kim came into the room and David punched her on the arm, hard, then shot her a sneer, turned, and stomped away. Merry concentrated on her French toast. In her dream, David hadn't been ten. He'd been wearing the same beautiful, worn, toast-colored leather bomber.

He was just embarrassed.

And so was Kim. "He never used to be like this. He's an ass," Kim told Merry. "He got like this after he started dating girls in Deptford. My mom says they're . . . you know."

Merry knew what Kim meant by "you know." But she hoped that David would wait for her instead of settling for anyone else, "you know" or not.

DOUBLE VISIONS
DOUBLE VISIONS

Mallory did play in the last few games of her indoor soccer season, but with what the coach saw as a halfhearted effort.

He understood entirely.

Finally, a rumor came along more alluring than the fire—about Christina Pell, a junior at Ridgeline Memorial, whose grandfather owned both the town banks. Christina came back late from Christmas break not because she had a serious case of flu but because of a more disgusting reason involving you-know-what.

It grabbed everyone's attention.

Mallory was sorry for Christina, but what an idiot! Still, at least no one talked about her or Merry anymore. But Mallory still didn't feel like herself, and hard as she tried, she couldn't act like her old self, either.

One day after one of the first outdoor practices, wenchy Trevor

Solwyn, who nobody liked except that having a tall forward was a big bonus, made a remark she pretended was supposed to be a whisper, but was actually meant for everyone to hear. Mally was a midfielder whose speed and accuracy made her an asset in any position except the goal, where her small size was a disability. But her ability to "see" the whole field now was impaired, as was her speed and timing. Her shots careened wide or smacked into the goalie's hands. When she pivoted, it took seconds instead of instants. Once the master of the fake, she now basically demonstrated her intentions to everyone else on the field, and everyone else blocked her. She ran as though her legs weighed as much as sandbags. Trevor said Mally should no longer be known by her nickname—the Hitter—but instead be called the Quitter.

Mally had never cried in public.

But now, she wheeled and ran off, pushing her arms through the sleeves of her parka and grabbing her boots as she ran. The coach tried, but couldn't catch up with her. He intended to tell Mally that her position as a starter for the Ridgeline Eighty-Niners—an elite traveling team formed in 1989 and comprised of girls from seventh grade through twelfth—was secure. He wanted to tell her to pay no attention to Trevor's poor sportsmanship, that he would speak to Trevor. After ten years of coaching, it still amazed him that people could be jealous even when someone got attention for a tragedy.

She vanished before he could find her.

Well, with a girl, you were probably better off letting her have her privacy, he thought.

Mallory was sitting against the outside fence that encircled the baseball field, the hood of her parka pulled up over her face, when Eden Cardinal sat down beside her. Besides Drew, Eden was the closest thing Mally had to a real friend. They didn't really *talk* talk, like text each other, they were just nicer to each other than they were to other people on the team. When they were changing or warming up, Eden would make a point of asking Mally some question about her home or her training, one you could tell she made up just to be polite.

Eden lived outside of town on a farm that made casual use of the name. Mallory saw it once, when Tim picked up Eden and several other girls for a game. It was really just sort of a large, crooked plot cut out of the woods, with about five houses in various states of disrepair, in which lived about ten brothers and sisters and about thirty cousins, uncles, and aunts.

Now she knew Eden was going to try to be kind, and Mally wanted no one's pity. So she huddled deeper into her hood. Eden seemed to ignore Mallory's efforts to avoid her.

"Trevor's a nasty wench," Eden said. "But she's noticing something. You're not yourself, Mal. And I don't mean on the field."

"I don't feel like myself. You wouldn't, either. And I don't think myself was ever so great."

"A lot of people are miserable after they go through something like you guys did, a long time after the wounds heal. I have an uncle who was in Vietnam. Maybe it's that . . ."

"I've only heard somebody say that about forty times," Mallory told her. "Maybe I just suck at soccer now. Isn't that possible?"

"There's one thing. You never used to put yourself down, Mally."

"You have me confused with Meredith Brynn. I'm not the self-esteem queen. If I didn't knock myself, I don't know why," Mallory answered. "At least the fire could have burned my freckles off." She tried to laugh and hiccuped instead.

"Mally, I think you have . . . like what people who were in wars have. Like my uncle has, only it made him a drunk. You're over it in your body, but not your head."

"It's not that."

"What is it?"

"You wouldn't get it. It's insane."

Eden sighed. "You'd be surprised," she said. "I so-called 'get' a lot of stuff you'd think is crazy, Mal."

"My sister . . ."

"Yeah?"

"When her bandages came off, her hands were great, given everything. The doctors were surprised that there's so little scarring."

"And this is bad why?" Eden asked.

"There's a little scarring, mostly on her palm, one long scar, like another lifeline. She grabbed a hot doorknob."

"But this is all good, Mal," Eden said.

"The fact that she has that scar means that we . . ." Mally began to cry, and once she did, the crying became sobbing, and the sobbing wouldn't stop. Soon she was shaking, snot running out of her nose, sleet mixing with tears in her eyes. She felt like a fool. Eden reached over and put her arms around Mallory.

"You poor little bit. Tell me. You what?"

"We're not the same anymore! It's like I'm not a twin! It's a spooky thing. . . ."

"I do understand. I don't mean about you being a twin. I don't understand *that*. But I know how you can hurt so bad over something that nobody else would think twice about," Eden said.

"Well, this is what it is. We're different now. We've been the same, totally the same except for her being right-handed, since . . . we were born . . . and it's separating us. . . ."

"Really? Or in your mind?"

"No, really."

"How do you know?" Eden asked.

"You won't believe this."

"I said . . . you know, Mally, not too much is strange to me. I'm an Indian," said Eden, and for the first time, Mallory made that connection, with Eden's long, straight black hair, her chiseled nose and cheekbones set up regally in her face, her perpetual tan.

"Okay. Identical twins . . . are just weird. Like, if Merry tripped and fell now, my knee would hurt. Not as bad as hers. But I would feel it."

"That must be incredible."

"It is. But we're used to it, so . . . it's just ordinary."

"But do you have the same thoughts?"

"No," Mally said. "But I can talk to her without saying anything. All twins can do that. I think. I guess. I really don't know any other twins. But I assume. I looked it up and it's called twin telepathy. It's not uncommon. Like people who are grown up and in different cities will buy each other the same birthday card, or get sick on the night their twin gets sick."

"That's amazing," Eden said. "But I believe it."

"Well, here's the thing. There's this other big part of it. And it's gone. Part of it is gone. We used to have the same dreams, at the same time. All our lives."

"You don't anymore."

"And not just that! She's an idiot! She's in love with David Jellico. . . ." Eden rolled her eyes, and Mally went on, "And I think he's a fake and a zero. It's like we're . . . two . . . we're . . ."

"Two different people. And only one of you feels alone."

"Right."

Eden stood and offered Mallory a hand up. "I think I'm glad you told me this. But I also think that I'm not the one you need to tell. You have to talk to Meredith. As for David, well, you know, Mal, the heart knows when things are right that seem wrong to everyone else."

Then Mallory stumbled, with a flash of the familiar-since-the-fire dizziness: In the instant of blackness, she saw a tall blond man, big through the shoulders. He was hiking, shouldering a huge pack, and on a ledge above him . . . what was that, with golden torch eyes, a huge wolf? A cougar?

"You . . . love somebody that you shouldn't," she blurted.

Eden said nothing. She reached out and pulled loose the thread of Mally's parka that had snagged on the chain-link fence when she'd stumbled, and tucked it back into the miniscule hole the fence had made. "That should be okay if you put a little stitch in it," she finally murmured.

"He's grown up. Is he in college?" Mally asked. Eden shook her head. "Does he work in the city? Edes, it's not fair you get to tell me all about my stuff and I say something about your stuff . . ."

"It creeps me out that you know," Eden finally told her.

"It's another thing."

"Another what thing?"

"Another thing since the fire. I can see other people's stuff. Like, not their names or junk. But I can see things. I thought they were hallucinations in the hospital, but I still have them. I see stuff David does, for one thing."

"He's a wilderness guide," said Eden.

Mallory swallowed back nausea. She had seen the man with the pack, and hadn't wanted to speak it aloud. Had she taken his image from Eden's mind? How could she know what was in *Eden's* mind? She had never seen anyone's thoughts except Meredith's, or things that had to do with Meredith. Not until now. What had broken into the house of her brain since the fire? Mallory didn't want it, any of it. It felt like licking someone else's skin.

She flashed again. The big cat . . . a mountain lion, white as farm butter.

"He's in danger in places where he goes," Mallory said softly to Eden. Eden fiddled with the catch on her big leather bag. The wind whickered about them, colder now as the sun set. "He really is."

"Not like you think," Eden finally answered calmly.

Mally thought, *What in the heck . . . ?*

"You know what I saw?" she asked.

"No," Eden said. "I'm just imagining. I'm trying to picture what you thought you saw from what I know. I'm not psychic."

"Neither am I!" Mallory told her.

"Are you sure?"

"Yes. But I saw an animal."

"That's not what you think, I told you," Eden said quickly, rummaging in her bag for her car keys. "I'm sure there are probably animals around him all the time," she added, as if they were talking about a strategy for defense against the Deptford Strikers. "I have to get home. My mom works third shift and I have to look after the kids. Want a ride?"

"From this one, this animal, he's in danger."

"Don't say that, Mallory." Eden looked alarmed.

"Okay." Mallory held up her hands. "Why?"

"It scares me."

"And not me? Like I wanted to see that?"

"He's not even out on the trail now."

"Cut it out! He is!"

"Not until next week."

"So I saw this guy, dressed in a blue flannel shirt over this long-sleeved waffle thing, a gray thing, with a . . . a red backpack . . . a tall guy with blond, no, like brownish blond hair, and black boots . . . and a red hat that has a lightning—"

"Stop it, Mally. Come on. I'll give you a ride. Jump in the sexy beast," Eden said nervously, pointing to her pickup truck, which seemed to have a dent in every possible flat surface. "He just got that hat. It was his birthday present from me. He's never even worn it. You must have seen one like it on someone else. That's all."

"I'll walk. My head is full of bees," Mally said. "I'll call my dad after a few minutes. He was going to pick me up anyhow. Thanks, Edes. For all that."

"I don't think I was much help," Eden said, but hurriedly now.

Mallory thought, *Why did I say that junk? Now I've scared her away. I could maybe have talked to her.*

Finally Mallory shrugged and said, "I don't think there is help. Maybe it's like you said and it will go away after I start forgetting the fire."

Eden smiled, but sadly.

ALONE IN THE MIRROR

ALONE IN THE MIRROR

That night, Mallory woke up crying. She turned her face into the pillow, trying to muffle the sound.

Meredith listened, knowing Mal would be furious if she said a word. It was she who got weepy. Finally, she turned on her reading lamp.

"You don't know, do you?" Mallory pleaded with her twin. "What's happening to us?"

"I don't know if it's something that would make me cry. We're growing up. What do you mean?"

"Merry, you didn't know I dreamed about the fire before it happened, and it wasn't because you weren't asleep."

"Yes it was."

"And you don't know what I was dreaming right now, do you?"

"I was awake."

"No you weren't. I heard you snoring about an hour ago."

"Okay, so I didn't know what you were dreaming."

"I was dreaming about David Jellico's circle of stones...."

"What?"

"His circle of shells or stones."

"How do you know about that?"

"I saw it."

"Mally, I didn't even know about that until, like, two weeks ago. What it is, is he has a graveyard for—"

"How did you know about it?"

"I, uh, dreamed about it," Merry admitted.

"So you know what it is."

"Not really," Merry lied.

"You do too," Mallory said evenly.

"Okay. It's a graveyard. For animals. Cats."

"And that's not all," said Mallory. "There was a girl with him...."

"Dee—"

"Not Deirdre. I saw another girl. And something else, too. Another person. A really old woman. She doesn't want him up there on the ridge."

Merry rubbed her arms. "She lives there?"

"I don't think she's . . . alive. You know she's dead, Mer."

"Okay, good night," Merry said, turning off the light. "You saw David Jellico with a ghost. Okay. Whatever."

"He goes there. He's going to go there . . . I don't know. Soon. It's just up from where I run. Just down the road from our camp."

"Shut up," said Meredith. "Laybite."

"You'll see her, too."

"BS. I don't see ghosties and freakies in my dreams."

"You will."

"Mallory," Meredith said. "I hate to tell you this, but I think you're semi-mentally ill. In a nice way. You're talking like a crazy person."

"And you think it's just, like, temporary, because of the fire." Mallory began to cry again. She didn't give a damn if Merry heard.

"We both feel strange," Merry said, getting up and sliding into bed next to Mallory, plumping her pillow at the foot of Mally's bed. "I didn't mean what I said."

"It's more than that. Maybe I am mentally ill. But I think it's something else."

"What, Ster?"

"Since the fire, I dream when . . . when I'm not asleep. And you don't know it."

Tears welled up in Merry's eyes. "I . . . don't. But I still hear you awake. I hear you when I listen for you. Mostly."

"Do you know why you don't see my dreams?"

"Not really."

"Because we're not the same anymore, Mer! Since before the fire . . ."

"We're still the same, Mallory."

"No, the scar on your hand. It's not ugly. But we're not—" She was about to say "the same person" when Meredith interrupted.

"We're still the same person."

"No! I feel all creepy, like I'm locked out of my own house."

"Ster, why don't I feel that way?"

"Maybe because you're dumb!" Mallory shouted—so loudly that Tim Brynn called out something muffled about it being a school night. "Maybe because you don't care about us the way I do."

"That's a sleaze thing to say! Why would you say that?"

"Maybe because it's true!"

"Mally! Are you crazy? You're my sister. You're, for God's sake, you're my best friend."

"Kim is your best friend. And Crystal and Sunny are your next best friends, and Alli and Erika after them! I don't want to be your friend. Everything is ruined."

Meredith knew that something Mallory was saying was entirely true. She decided to ignore it.

Instead, she struggled with what she had to find words for and finally blurted out, "You're my heart!" She had heard her father say this once to her mother. It seemed to be what she meant. She didn't know what else to say. And it didn't seem enough.

"Well, I didn't tell you everything. The girl I dreamed in the woods with David? It was you."

Meredith tried to conceal her delight, but failed. "Was I older?"

"I couldn't tell. You weren't taller! But you were running around like a little wood fairy and he was chasing you. You'd have loved it. It was totally stupid," Mallory said. "He's stupid!"

"He is not!"

"You don't know because you don't feel what I feel!"

"I never did feel everything you felt!"

"There's a difference between having different opinions and

thoughts and really feeling what the other person feels, Merry. On big stuff . . ."

"I know."

"Then why don't you care?"

"Ster, it's because . . ." Merry said slowly. "I don't think we can fix it."

Mallory sat up and threw her bolster, hard, at Merry's head. Merry threw it back. She whispered, "Mally, why are you mad at me for this?"

"I'm not," Mallory said, beginning to cry again. "I'm not mad at you! I'm just never going to feel normal again. And you will. I know it!"

"I won't if you don't."

"You will," Mallory insisted, "because you'll try to. You'll pretend you do until it's almost the same as if you really do. You'll just deny it."

"Why wouldn't I do that? I mean really, why? Why wouldn't I want to feel like I did before? Why wouldn't I want to be happy if I could? But I don't think it's going to go back, either. Truthfully. I don't think I'm going to feel the same."

Mally admitted, "Maybe you won't. Ever." She said then, "This wasn't supposed to be part of growing up."

"No," said Meredith. "This is like a bad joke."

But when she fell asleep, Merry dreamed of David, working in the same rock garden she'd seen in her hospital dream and the dream at Kim's overnight.

Then, just before she woke, she dreamed of an old woman,

with a sweet apple-doll face, and both hands out in front of her with the palms out, as if to hold Merry back. The woman shook her head firmly.

Merry woke up. Her head ached. She felt dizzy. She saw the old woman shake her head.

Once and again.

No.

Merry got up and jumped into the shower before it was hot.

She would not, would *not*, start having weird Mally posttraumatic flashback things.

She had to get up earlier now, to get dressed, even earlier than the usual hour before Mallory did—because her hands were still clumsy, especially with small things such as earrings. But when she came out of the shower, she saw that Mally was asleep. Not even up for her run.

She was fast asleep, and Meredith tried to jump into her twin's thoughts. She couldn't. She couldn't follow Mallory there.

The old lady. The old lady was real, but who was she? She wasn't at all frightening. If this was seeing a ghost . . .

Meredith wasn't afraid of ghosts. For all she knew, her ancestors lived near her in this house. Sometimes she sensed presences, soft touches, the scent of lavender and lilies of the valley. She would not have been frightened of them if they came and sat on her bed. She had "seen" her mother's lost car keys when she was small. She had "seen" Grandma dressing up to surprise Grandpa before Christmas dinner, so that when Merry came over, she knew where Grandma had dropped her earring. But she wasn't even sure how she felt about life after death. It was something she'd never thought all the way through. Why not? She supposed that was what Mally would call "shallow."

Well, now she would think. She would concentrate.

This old woman was supposed to have a message for Merry. *Stop.* But stop what?

Meredith glanced down at her sister. She reached out and touched the single pearl stud in Mally's ear. Mally twitched, but didn't waken.

Now *she* was upset! It never failed. Mally got into a thing . . . It was stupid to be so upset. After all, they were alive. The little kids were unhurt. Full function would return to Merry's hand. The doctor predicted she'd have no nerve damage, just some stiffness she'd work out in physical therapy. The scar on her palm would last forever, but grow fainter each year. Maybe this . . . distance would go away, too.

But what Mallory had said was true: She and her sister would never again have the same handprint.

And Mally blamed herself for all of it. Merry knew that.

She tried to think of something pleasant. Like the smell of David's leather jacket.

She went to the kitchen. Campbell was making pancakes.

"Why are you even up, Mom?" Merry asked. Campbell worked from five p.m. to five a.m., ten days straight, did an hour on the treadmill or outside, and hit the sack. At the end of the ten days, she got two straight weeks off. This was the end of the past ten days—Campbell's hard-earned mini-vacation.

"I don't know," Campbell said honestly. "I couldn't sleep."

"You love to sleep."

"So do you," Campbell said.

"Well, I have stuff going on."

"I heard Mallory yelling. What's up?"

"We had a fight."

"A regular fight?" Campbell asked.

"We don't have regular fights anymore," Merry admitted. "It's all so . . . intense with her." She asked, "Can I have some coffee?"

"No," Campbell replied automatically.

"Maybe we should get separate rooms," Merry said then.

"Now that would really work out," Campbell replied, shaking her head. "Your dad would knock out a wall, and I'd kill myself painting, and then you'd both sleep in the same room anyhow."

"Right now, I'd live in a different country," Merry told her.

"So it was a serious and also abnormal fight."

"I don't know."

"Does Mallory feel guilty about your hand?" Campbell asked.

"Yes." Merry puffed out her lips. "Sort of. Were you eavesdropping on us?"

"No, you were screaming. Please. These walls are thick, but not that thick. So it's more than just regular guilt," Campbell went on, setting a short stack down in front of Meredith. Campbell's sister, Amy, sent them syrup from Vermont, where Amy had a summerhouse. Merry knew she was inhaling carbs, but couldn't resist. Campbell sat down with her and took a plate of three cakes, too. "She feels a debt. It's a pretty common psychological thing. People get mad at someone when they owe them more than they can ever pay back."

"You said it was posttraumatic stress before."

"Maybe it was, before. Anyhow, do you want to talk about it?" she asked.

"You wouldn't get it, Mom."

"I wouldn't get it as a twin, but I'd get it as a mother."

"But not all of it."

"Look, fine, then. All I'm saying is . . . my mother used to tell me nothing ever got worse by talking about it. You don't have to."

"What's the point? You would never know how I feel."

"That's what Gwenny said."

"What's Grandma got to do with this?" Merry asked.

"Just, when you were born, she said there would be things about you I would never understand, even more than other mothers and kids. Maybe she would get it. She's a twin."

"She's not a twin."

"She is. Or was. Her twin sister died when they were kids your age."

"Really?" Merry said, her eyes widening. "Grandma never said."

"It still hurts her. That's probably why. But you could still try to explain it," Campbell said. "When someone is part of you, you don't like to see her this way. When someone is part of your own body, you hurt for her."

"Maybe you do get it," Meredith said, glancing up. She had been slicing her pancakes into strips of eight, then cutting them into smaller strips of sixteen. "That is how we feel."

Campbell said sadly, "Merry, I meant you and me. I meant Mally and you and me. That you girls are part of me."

"Oh," Meredith said. Now she had hurt her mom. "It's not like we don't love you, Mom."

"I know that," Campbell answered. "You're wasting that food. I made it from scratch, not a mix. Why don't you try eating a bite?" Merry did. It was cold. "So?" Campbell prompted her.

"Well, we dream the same things."

"I know that. You used to sleepwalk and talk about them."

"We did?"

"When you were two or three."

"Now we don't anymore."

"Don't sleepwalk?"

"Don't have the same dreams at the same time."

"Ah, well. Maybe it's just a temporary thing. Does it bother you? Does Mally mind more than you?"

"She minds more than I do, but I would mind more if I let myself think about it," Merry said. "It used to be like being in the same . . . *mmm* . . . airplane. Like, you could look out the windows and talk to other people, but you were always going the same place and you could always see where the other one was."

"And now you can't."

"Not when we're asleep."

"But you *sleep* when you're asleep," Campbell said helplessly. "Although I have to say, part of why I stayed up is that you look like you haven't been sleeping that much."

"Do I look gross?" Merry asked, nearly dropping her fork.

"No! Just tired."

"You know the old joke. When people say you look good, they mean you lost weight. When they say you look tired, they mean you look like . . ."

"Like crap," said Campbell. "I know the joke."

Tim came into the kitchen, poured his coffee, kissed Merry's and Campbell's heads, and wandered out to the car.

"I never know how Dad gets to work when he's basically still asleep," Merry said.

"Me either. Thank God for seat belts," Campbell said. "So this dreaming thing . . ."

"It's not just dreaming now, but when we're not—"

They both looked up, as if they'd heard a crash, an impact of silence. Mallory stood in the doorway, dressed for school, her face linen white, her eyes shadowy.

"Laybite," she told Merry softly.

Merry got up.

"Mommy, Drew's honking!" Meredith said, her face pinched with fear and anxiety.

"Girls, wait . . . I'll drive you both in."

"No, Mom. I have a test first hour," Mallory said, and was out the door.

Merry shrugged and followed.

Campbell noticed that Merry had left her cheerleading bag, her prized green-and-white JV Ridgeline duffel, on the floor, for the first time since she had earned it, a year before. She stood up to run after her, but Drew was already passing their house on the way down the road toward school. Mallory sat in front, not speaking, staring straight ahead. Merry was in back, her head against the seat, her eyes closed.

As soon as they were out of sight of the house, Drew glanced at Mally. "Put your belt on, Brynn," he said, longing to touch her hand. You didn't do that with Mallory, though. "What's wrong with you?"

"Didn't sleep."

"How come?"

"Storm kept me up," she said.

There wasn't a drop on Drew's car. The old grooved places in the sidewalks were dry. "I slept right through it. Must have been a bad one, to wake you up," he said.

Merry answered, without opening her eyes, "It was."

MEETING PLACES

MEETING PLACES

With Caitlin Andersen in her proper place *behind* her, Meredith took her stance for "No More Take Backs," their cheer dance at the Big Twist Junior Invitational.

It had gotten them this far.

Ridgeline was third in the competition, on the second day. All the parents had come along and spent the evening in the restaurant of the fancy hotel next to the conference center in Donovan, a ritzy town two hours upstate. Merry and Mallory had been up half the night, ordering room-service Caesar salads and riding the elevators with the other cheerleaders, twenty-five teams from all over New York. For once, Mally forgave her sister for being a fake athlete and joined in the craziness. She didn't even seem to mind the choruses of "I'm so sure" and "I was like . . . so what?"

They'd probably stayed up too late, Merry thought.

She was tired. Her reactions were probably slower than they

should have been. But adrenaline was a beautiful thing. And she'd had two cups of strong tea with lunch.

Ahead of them were the Donovan Eagles from a richie prep school out on Long Island. In first were the girls Merry had to admit were better—the girls from PS 15, in Spanish Harlem. They were not only better, they were better-looking, too. The Donovan Eagles were almost neck and neck with the PS 15 Rockets in school cheers and quad routines. And when it came to dance, the girls from PS 15 blew both Merry's squad and the preps out of the water. Solid tumblers all, Merry's squad needed a rhythm transfusion. Plus, there were three or four girls on Ridgeline's team who were . . . well, Merry would never say gross, but a little thick. Like, couldn't get a thigh boot on to save their lives. The long-haired girls from the city made Merry feel like some kind of black-haired leprechaun, in her cheesy green-and-white uniform that was new about a year before Merry was born. The Donovan girls had probably snipped the tags off their teal-and-gray sweaters that morning before the first round.

She would have to pull off something amazing.

She knew what it was.

Anyone could do a mount to a lib if she had speed and balance, but hardly anyone could do a front flip dismount. Merry could. She and Kellen, with Caitlin and Kim as spotters, had practiced it in secret before winter break. But could she do it in competition after two months off, when she'd been back in action for only a few weeks?

She and the others sprinted out onto the floor.

As they took their places for practice before the music began, Merry looked up and, in the stands, she saw David. Had he driven all the way from Ridgeline to this big convention hotel two hours from their house just to see Kim compete?

Or to see her?

To see *her*?

Merry's heart thudded, the way her mother once described it— like a bird in the cage of her ribs.

"Can you do it?" she asked Kim and Kellen as they warmed up for the morning finals. "Just like we practiced? After the catch you put me into a stand, and I know I can land it."

"I'm not doing it unless we tell the others," Sunday Scavo spoke up. "Because we could all get kicked off."

"Not if we win."

"Duh. If we win, and you get hurt . . . it's all of our butts," Sunday said. She waved at her parents. Merry couldn't understand how Sunday could even speak to her parents, who had named her Sunday River Scavo after the ski resort where they were when she was conceived—my God! It was disgusting. She wondered what her name would be: Juneberry? Sugar Maple? You only had to count backward to figure out her parents had been at the family camp one spring weekend, at one of the cabins, which were all named for New England trees, when they got the idea that resulted in her and her sister. Campbell and Tim didn't go for weekends to the cabin camp anymore, not since Tim bought the store.

But they always went in summer! And Adam—come to think of it, which she did not want to, Adam was born in April, nine months after their July vacation. At least she didn't have to think about her parents doing it more than once a year.

The first-place team was performing to "Beautiful, Beautiful Girl," letter perfect, every move crisp as a flag in a stiff breeze. Left hurkey. Right hurkey. Huge, huge kicks. Big synchronized jumps. Sexy, sexy contortion moves. Double backovers, endlessly. Merry watched in agony. The one thing they lacked was a super flyer— and Merry's team lacked one, too.

They lacked Merry.

"Listen, Kim, Sunny, Crystal, Caitlin, Mimi! All you guys. Kellen and I have to do this! They're gonna take this away! We've worked for this for two years! This is our last year before high school!" She looked from face to face. "We all want to get moved up to varsity as freshmen! Don't we? I can do this. Full forward pike after the catch. We just don't do the final stand. We do this instead."

She planned a dismount so daring it would either wow the judges or get her squad disqualified. What Merry had going for her was how much more cheerleaders were getting away with in competition now—from uniforms with strings of lights built into the see-through tops to purple faux-hawks and navel rings. What she had against her was tradition. Either way, she thought, they might as well go down in glory, and walk away with the chops if not the trophy. She would perform the stunt just the way she and Kellen and Kim had in their little after-practice practice sessions.

After she did her stand on top of the pyramid, one leg extended, then dropped into the basket, Kellen and Sunny would go into a lunge and lift her onto their knees. From their shoulders she would do a forward flip—like a dismount from a balance beam—and land (well, hopefully) on the gym floor.

The problem was, this kind of move wasn't permitted for cheer-leaders in competition in Merry's age group.

The problem was that their knees were higher and even unsteadier than a balance beam and there was no mat underneath. Coach killed her every time she saw Merry do that move, or a twist catch, or anything she wasn't supposed to be doing. But when Coach yelled at her, it was almost like the way you yelled at a little kid, half laughing as you did it.

"Coach Everson says she's told you no upside down, not even in high school," said Sunday. "Only college. It's, like, illegal."

Crystal Fish, with one leg extended in standing splits against the concrete wall of the practice gym, said, "Please, Coach would slaughter us. You just started back *not even two months* ago. You're her little doll face. If you hit your hand, we'll be toast. Include me not."

"We'll be able to catch her no problem and once she's in the stand, I'll give her help going over," said Kellen Fish, Merry's anchor and Crystal's big brother. Kellen was a freshman.

"Then we can both get killed," Crystal said placidly. "That would wipe out our whole family."

"Listen," Merry begged. "We need to do this! Otherwise . . . we just don't have anything. The girls from P.S. 15 actually should win, because they had to sell Sally Snax to even buy their uniforms. They get the sympathy vote. And the other girls probably don't even have to go to class for weeks before a meet. You know, private school rules?"

"Merry . . . don't make us get in trouble. It's just a meet," said Kim.

"And like we won't have ten more next year," Crystal said languidly. "I plan on living to be twenty. Your units up there in the old bleachers will kill us if coach doesn't. No way, Mer."

"Way, Fish. I'm the captain!"

Crystal looked at Meredith as though she were a little bug. Then she lowered her beautiful, ballet-turned leg and said, "You are CO-captain. With me, Brynn. It's your competition. Your loss. Coach will kick you out. I mean, out for good. You'll have to start wearing stripper outfits like the Pom Pom girls."

"It's not fair! You had all your meets when I just got to sit there!" Merry cried, bursting into tears. "You cheered for basketball when they went to third in state for the first time! Now I get my last chance and you're just going to crap out on me? Come on. I can land this. Me and Kim and Caitlin and Kellen have done it dozens of times. Dozens. Coach even knows."

"And she's fine about it, right?" Crystal asked.

"No, but she knows about it," Merry said.

She glanced up at Coach Everson, who had taken her place kneeling in front of the stage according to the rules. Coaches were not allowed to speak to the girls for ten minutes before they competed. But Coach was watching the conversation with a sharp eye, as though she knew something was up.

"She knows about it," Kim repeated, trying to back Merry up, but leery of Coach Everson's look, which seemed to be boring holes in her back. Kim glanced between Merry and the rest of the group. Alli seemed to be on Merry's side. So did Caitlin.

But Crystal was like a power queen. You could almost see lightning come out of her fingernails. She looked mad, and Crystal's mad was like anyone else's crazy.

Merry dialed down.

"Listen," Merry said, sensing she was pushing too hard. "I have a better idea. I'll do a full-split in the air, a toe-touch dismount, from you guys' shoulders. But we won't stop there. We'll do something else. Caitlin, you can do a back-flip from a standstill. Alli, you can! You do two in a row into a split. And I'll do something else. Let's go then. Everybody! Competition smiles! Ridgeline spirit! Let's run the gauntlet." The girls and Kellen formed a double line, Merry grabbed Alli's hand and ran through, followed by all the others until they leapt into line. When they reached the end, the whole squad shouted, "Ridgeline Rockets! Dream team!" Meredith, pumped her fist.

As they ran out, Crystal whispered, "You watch it. I mean it. You'll be in another coma if we get in trouble!" Crystal said. "You won't be responsible. You'll be in the newspaper again for most comas in a six-month period. Probably on CNN."

In the stands, Mallory told her parents, "She's going to get caught in the basket *and* she's thinking she'll do a pike out of it, like off a balance beam. Be prepared."

Tim and Campbell stood up to stop her; but the first notes of "No More Take Backs" had already begun.

"Don't flip out," Mallory said. "If she was going to get big-time hurt, I'd know it."

"You mean, you'd know it in a weird twin way? Is she going to get little time hurt?" Tim yelled over the noise.

Mally shrugged. She pretended to shake a toy eight-ball in her hands. "My sources say no." She laughed. "Come on, Dad. I know it because I'm her sister and I can tell when she's trying to be all goody-goody when she's really being sneaky. I can tell because I heard them say they'd do it if they weren't in first after the early rounds. Duh."

"This isn't a joke Mallory," Campbell said, in the voice usually followed by *you're-grounded*.

But she had to look away then. Down on the floor, the routine was going like silk.

"Step and step," Merry said quietly. "Kick, kick. One, two, three, jump. One, two, three, down on four, up, five six," she gave David her most glistening smile. He smiled, with a hint of a nod. "Hip, Hip, shake it. Hip, hip, shake it, last time," Meredith went on. "Now down on your knees . . ." The girls next ran forward, and slid to the floor. In a line, they slipped into synchronized forward rolls, next jumping to their feet and performing a few steps of of hip-hop, ending in a high toe-kick. The whole line then dropped to their knees and knelt on all fours. Beginning with Crystal at the far left, each cheerleader used the girl next to her as a chair: With her back balanced on the back of the girl beneath her, Caitlin, Alli, Sunny and the others lay back and did horizontal splits in the air. When they traded places for a second series of splits, each motion sharp and on the beat, it had a stylish silhouette effect Coach liked to call "the Rockettes,"—although most of the girls had never heard of the most famous kick line in America.

Meredith said, "Okay last time. Now ready . . ."

To either side, Sunday and Mimi went up to their two-legged stands, their feet planted on the knees of the sturdier girls. Kellen and Kim hoisted Alli and Crystal to the second tier and they pulled Merry and Caitlin to the top of the pyramid, where all three first stood with both arms and then one leg extended.

The crowd cheered and the prep-school girls tapped their toes impatiently.

"Now, let's do it!" Merry instructed them.

With a moment of hesitation she hoped wasn't obvious, Merry dropped from her mount into the basket formed by Kim and Kellen. Then she was standing on Kellen's and Kim's sturdy hands. Even she was aghast at the fear factor. She'd never done a full-split toe-touch dismount. But seven years of gymnastics paid off as Kellen and Kim helped Meredith get the height and do the classy dismount. At her side, she saw Alli and Caitlin drop off their top tier, then face away from the crowd.

They did two consecutive back flips into a full split.

But Merry did a front flip, a back flip and landed in a horizontal split, waving at the crowd like a madwoman.

So she hadn't done the full pike she'd planned in the gym.

They'd have lost points for it anyhow.

By the way the judges were smiling at her, she knew she'd done enough.

All old people, like the coaches, remembered that old Nadia Comenici move from the Romanian gymnastics team of about 1904.

They'd departed from the plan, but that wasn't a cause for a points deduction.

Merry signed happily. Dream team perfect.

Of course, her mother would be having a bird about the split dismount—technically, you could break a leg—but if she fled away from the trophy ceremony before her family could make it down out of the stands . . . Hi. Smile. Smile. Big trophy. Hand it to Crystal.

Bye Bye. She was off toward the bus.

"Hotdog beach," said one of the girls from Prep World with a glamorous platinum sneer.

Even one of the four judges had to stop herself from applauding. She quickly glanced around with a guilty gaze before bending over her clipboard. But then all four of the judges bent to confer. Merry bit her lip. She knew they were going to be docked for an illegal move. But she knew that in their hearts, judges were hotdoggers, too. They had to be impressed.

Campbell wanted to be angrier than she was. But all around her, athletes—even boys—were cheering for these little girls who had turned a sissy pastime into a demonstration of raw guts and power. How mad could she get?

Merry watched the judges closely. From the judges' body language, the Ridgeline Rockets knew the cup was theirs, but they could only stand politely, in rest stand, until the verdict was final. People in the stands were screaming, on their feet.

"Did you see that little girl?" a father called out.

"She's my daughter!" Tim roared. Campbell elbowed him in the ribs.

Campbell stood up and began shouting, in a voice she hoped Merry could hear, that Meredith wouldn't be leaving the house until summer. Merry sneaked a glance at her coach. Becky Everson had her hands in her pockets and was looking down at the toes of her shoes. But finally, she seemed to decide that it would improve appearances if she was behind her squad, win or lose. Slowly, Coach began to applaud, too. She would give Merry a lecture. But she admired her guts.

The judges stood.

After the announcement of the winners and the victory cheer, Kim came running and lifted Merry off the ground. "My total hero!" she said. "The flying shrimp rides again!"

David appeared behind his sister and said, "Some move, Meredith."

"Just for you!" Merry giggled, flipping one of her hands in a parody of her crowd wave.

"Too bad you're a baby girl, shrimp," David said, and Kim punched him.

Meredith could have fainted with pure joy.

Will Brent seemed to shrink in her mind to a little mannequin, and then to a concept. She saw her parents approaching, with Campbell literally shaking her fist.

"Run!" Merry yelled. "Here come my parents! See you at home! Love you, Mom! I gotta make the bus!" Campbell broke into a fast trot, but Merry lost herself in the crowd.

"You'll never catch her," Mallory told her mother.

"She was pretty amazing," Tim admitted.

"She's practically a convalescent!" Campbell said.

"I just said she was pretty amazing. She's got a lot of guts. You can't deny her that, Cam."

"It's because she has this big crush on Kim's brother," Mallory told them. Adam stuck a finger down his throat and mimed gagging.

"That's absurd," Campbell said. "She's a child, and he must be seventeen."

"He's sixteen," said Mallory. "I agree with Adam."

"I'm five years older than you are," Tim reminded Campbell, mussing her hair.

"Shut up," Campbell said. "That was a different time. . . ."

"Pioneer times," said Adam.

"You, too," Campbell told him. She was disgruntled. "This ruins the whole trophy thing. Why did she take such a chance? And David Jellico? Bonnie would kill him if he's encouraging her. It's ridiculous. She's thirteen!"

"I'm hungry," said Adam.

Campbell did a quick inventory. The crowd was shoving her forward toward the doors. Astonishingly, Adam was still wearing both his gloves. She could feel the lump of her leather driving gloves in her own pocket, hear the sharp jingle of her keys. Tim's sleepy, goofy grin told her that she would be driving home. And she didn't want to spend two hours waiting to get out of the parking lot. Grabbing Adam's hand, she broke into a trot, calling back that she'd get the van and pick Mally and Tim up. Her phone vibrated. She snapped it open. Meredith! The little minx. She was apologizing in advance. Well. It had been a lousy few months for Merry. She deserved this. Campbell typed back, *Congrats, brat.*

No one noticed that Mallory had stopped and was slumped against the school wall, panting, her lips pale. Tim was still talking with her, talking through the routine as if she were a step behind him, pointing out that though his heart was in his stomach when he saw Merry dismount, he secretly knew she could do it. Tim said, "You don't think your dad's so old, do you, Mal? Adam? Where's Adam? Oh, he went with Mom. You know I can still beat *you* one-on-one . . . Mallory? Mal?"

He whirled and sprinted back up the long hall. Fifty feet ahead of them, Campbell heard him and started to fight her way back through the crowd. People were still talking about Meredith: *Did you see that short, little girl flip? Isn't it something what kids can do now?* No one seemed to notice Mallory at all.

Sweeping Mallory up in his arms, Tim crouched against the concrete wall and called out to Campbell, "What is it? Look at her, please?"

"Sit down," said Campbell. All of them sat down on the floor of the hall. Her eyes on her watch, she laid her fingers against Mallory's wrist. "She's sweating. Her pulse is racing. I don't know what's wrong with her. Mally? Are you sick to your stomach?"

"No," said Mallory. How could she explain? How could she explain the waking dream that had gone streaking across her mind like a sped-up snippet of film?

She could as easily explain the composition of the rings of Saturn to an infant.

What she could ask, finally, was, "Is Merry taking the bus? Or did she ride with Kim?"

"I know she's on the bus. She just sent me a little text message! I assume that Kim is, too," Campbell said. "What's this got to do with Merry?"

"I really, really did see it, then," Mallory whispered.

For the second time in three months, which also was the second time in her life, Mallory fainted.

"She's fine," said Dr. Staats. "If I had to guess, this is stress-related or hormonal. We'll take a little blood and check for a virus. She's got a lot going on. Puberty can be weird." Mallory sat glumly on the paper sheet of the examining table. She wished, not for the first time that night, that a high-tension wire would fall on her and twist her into a little black pencil of ash. If humiliation could kill you, she'd be dead ten times in the past ten minutes. Adam sat in the corner, with the twisted fingers of a rubber glove hanging from his nostrils, grinning and letting his tongue loll out. *He might be stupid*, thought Mallory, *but he knows what puberty is.*

The beauty of Ridgeline was in things such as this—a doctor who would leave home late on a Saturday afternoon and unlock the clinic personally because a child she'd delivered was in trouble. Dr. Staats was at the clinic before Campbell wheeled into the parking lot. When Campbell saw the doctor's familiar car, a snazzy vintage Corvette, she exhaled with relief.

"Can Adam please leave?" Mallory begged. "Please? He's acting retarded and making me nuts."

"Take him outside, Tim," Campbell said. Reluctantly, covertly grabbing a few more surgical gloves as he passed, Adam followed his father out into the waiting room. Mallory supposed she should be grateful for Dr. Staats coming over to the clinic on her day off. Campbell insisted at first that they stop at the nearest urgent care; Mallory protested so loudly that her father jumped and Campbell swerved: If she *had* to see a doctor—and she did *not* have to see a doctor—then it was going to be *her* doctor, though this was absurd because she was fine and all she wanted to do was go home and why didn't anyone get that?

And then, suddenly, in what seemed to all of them to be the middle of her rant, Mallory fell asleep and didn't wake up until they were in the Ridgeline Medical Specialists parking lot. Although she couldn't know, this would be the pattern: the lurid picture, colored like a bad movie in shaky cam, slammed against her visual field, the faint, the hysteria—then sleep.

"Mally, have you ever had a blackout before?" Dr. Staats asked.

"Not like this," Mallory said. "It wasn't exactly a blackout. I passed out during the fire. This was just . . . I can't explain it. It was like a shock."

"Like something frightened you?"

Yes, Mallory thought. *Like something frightened me. And I'd love to tell you what but you'd put me in the hospital for going psycho. Which I probably actually am.*

"Sometimes when people enter puberty, hormonal changes . . ." the doctor began.

"It wasn't that," Mallory answered. "I know it wasn't."

"You might not feel developed in other ways," Campbell began.

Mallory put her hands over her ears.

"Oh, please kill me," she said through her teeth. "Doctor Staats, have you met my mother? My mother is a nurse! We've had the changes-in-a-woman's-body conversation about every Thursday since I was nine years old. It's right before the if-you-ever-need-birth-control-you-know-you-can-tell-me conversation. I've never even kissed a boy. Please!" Mally pleaded. "I'd know if I were having my period. Or a mood swing. Or anything. And if I was, Meredith would be having it, too. Maybe we should go home. What if Merry fainted, too, Mom? What if she's on the kitchen floor and hit her head?"

"I called her. She's fine," said Campbell.

Great, Mally thought. The least Meredith could do was go crazy at the same time.

"She's just worried about you. Kim is there with her."

Kim? Mallory thought. *Oh, no, please no, I can't talk to her with Kim there!*

So Mallory concentrated on how to get Kim out of their house, or at least out of earshot, while Dr. Staats and Mally's mother talked for about six hours about possible reasons for Mallory's dizziness, from low blood sugar to an ear infection. Finally, Dr. Staats patted Campbell's arm, gave her a lab slip, and promised to rush the blood work through.

Mally thought she would scream if she didn't get out of the room.

She didn't want to tell Merry what she'd seen.

But she had to.

Who else was there?

She thought of Eden. No. Eden was a high-school girl, a basically normal, decent person. Mallory had already creeped her out once. She thought of Drew. She longed for Drew. But did she really want her only true friend to think she was nuts?

Mallory just knew that Merry had blabbed something to Kim and she was furious. How much had Merry told about what was happening to them? No matter what she'd said, it was too much. It was dangerous—especially with Kim! The fewer people who knew, the better. She flipped open her cell phone and texted Merry: *Lts tlk wen I gt hm. Aln. K?* She hoped she wasn't interfering with the monitors for someone stroking out somewhere else in the clinic. It said right on the front door that cell phones were not allowed. No. She remembered now. The clinic was closed. They were the only ones there.

Campbell, watching, would have assumed Mallory could simply call Merry on the telepathy beeper. But was that working anymore? Did that work only if both of them had it turned on or if a crisis slammed through whatever else one of them was thinking or doing? She could ask Merry, but Mally was too fierce. Mally would clam up.

As for Mally, this wasn't something she wanted to talk about with Merry *except* if it were face-to-face and with words.

It was like a dream; but it wasn't a dream.

It was, she supposed, a vision. Like the vision she'd had with Eden.

But why?

Why then, why just—blam!—walking down the concrete hall that led to the convention center parking lot? What were they even talking about? Adam said he was hungry. Then Adam took off with Mom. Her father was talking about Merry running off with Kim, and about how great Merry was, and how great Tim was . . . but it wasn't about Tim. Kim.

That was it!

Her mother got all pissed that Meredith had a crush on David, how Bonnie would be mad if David liked Merry, too.

David Jellico.

And what would her mother say if Mally just blurted it out right now: *I saw your best friend's son kill a dog. I saw it. I saw him hang a dog on a tree until it died.*

She had to see Merry. It was probably better that Merry wasn't home alone, she thought. But what did it matter? If Kim was there and David showed up, they'd ask him in without even thinking about it. They'd make him hot chocolate. *Oh, come on!* Maybe she was only mad at David. Maybe she was jealous of Merry's crush on David and not admitting her own feelings. That was it. No, that wasn't it. David was an ass. But not a dangerous ass. Just an immature jerk. But where was David? Right now?

If only there was a way she could put her hands over the eyes of her brain, and stop seeing it over and over and over.

It was too pitiful and awful. She had to be some kind of lunatic even to think about it. A black-and-white dog, middle-sized, with a ruff on its throat, its legs clawing the air, its mouth dripping foam, a rope around its poor neck, and David (*It couldn't be David!*) slowly pulling the rope higher and higher off the ground, over the branch of a tree. She knew the dog. She had seen that dog before. Mallory tried again to wish the picture from her brain. This was going to happen, actually happen. That much she knew for sure. Her heart began to thud, and her breathing came in gasps.

"Are you feeling faint again?" Campbell asked.

"No, Mom. I'm fine. I'm totally starving, though," Mally said, trying to sound like a normal whiny teenager. "I'm tired of sitting here." God! She had to pretend and see this, too? The movie burst across her mind again. Rocks and trees. Something else in the background—a hill, a cliff? She recognized it, but she couldn't think. She didn't know where the freaking place was. "Mom, Dr. Staats, I didn't have anything to eat since breakfast. I was nauseated at lunch from all the junk we ate in the hotel last night. And then I got hungry but the lines were too long at the concession stand at the meet. That's what's really getting to me. It has to be."

"Okay, we'll get your blood drawn and then go to Friendly's," said Campbell.

"I want you to make me grilled cheese at home. The special way," Mally said. "I can have my blood drawn tomorrow. I just want to go to home. Please, Mom?"

"You always wanted grilled cheese when you were little and had a cold," Campbell said, stroking Mallory's hair. Mally felt like some kind of big emotional turd. She was lying right to her mother's face and being phony sweet about it, too.

"Yes, Mommy," said Mallory, barely able to talk around a lump of self-hatred. But Campbell was undone by Mallory's gentle appeal.

"Okay," Campbell said. "We'll go home."

But when Mallory's feet hit the porch, she was running for her bedroom, as Campbell called out for her in vain.

"Listen! Trophy princess!" Mally said, taking Merry's cell out of her hand and snapping it closed. "Where's Kim?"

"She had to go home. Her grandparents are coming over. What

is up with you? You just hung up on William." It was Merry's new name for Will—part of their semireconciliation. Merry thought it made both of them sound older.

As if, Mallory thought.

She said, "I don't care if I hung up on *Prince* William. Who I know you think David Jellico looks like. Listen to this. David is going to kill a dog."

"Uh, Mal, you have to excuse me. You have me confused with someone from your planet."

"He's going to kill a dog, and . . . and it's the . . . it's the Scavos' border collie, Pippen. I thought of it on the way home. It's Sunny Scavo's dog. I know it is."

"You're out of your mind."

"Merry. I wish I were. I don't have any idea why this is happening and why the same thing isn't happening to you. All I know is that this hasn't happened yet, but it's going to."

"Did a little voice tell you?" Merry asked, casually opening her flip phone.

"No. There was no . . . sound at all," Mallory said, her eyes filling with tears. "I just knew, like the fire, that it was real and it was going to happen. I just spent an hour in the doctor's office, Merry. When I saw this, I fainted! Ask Mom." She didn't realize she was yelling.

"She fainted," Campbell called from the bottom of the stairs. "Do you still want grilled cheese? Cheddar or Swiss?"

"Swiss," called Merry. "Make mine a little burny."

Campbell hollered back, "I wasn't asking you, Meredith! I'll make your butt a little burny, miss. You know you weren't sup-posed to do any stunts. . . ." Campbell sprinted up the stairs.

"Mom, the doctor said I should eat," Mallory reminded her mother quietly.

"I know. Shoot! I'll deal with you later," Campbell told Mer-edith. "I'm not forgetting."

Both girls sat rigid with tension until their mother was out of earshot.

"I can't believe they would ground me for doing something right," Merry said mournfully.

"Please! How can you think about that now? How can you think about cheerleading? This could already be happening! I'm not kidding," Mally said as soon as she could shut their door. "Call Kim. Ask where David is."

"No."

"Then I will."

"No."

Mallory took out her own cell phone. "I'll tell her what I think, too."

"Go ahead," Meredith said, setting her jaw. She looked at Mallory then. Mallory looked half out of her mind. This was serious. She felt the wall fall down.

"Call Sunny, then," Mallory begged. She slapped the phone so that it went clattering into the corner. "Call her!"

"Okay, okay. Don't have a bird," said Meredith.

"What are you fighting about?" Tim called up the stairs. "Your mother is down here making cheese sandwiches and you two are up there screeching like cats. Get your big mouths down here. Mer-edith? Mallory?" They ignored him, knowing he would wander away in a moment's time.

A few moments later, Mally listened as Meredith asked for Sunny Scavo.

"She is? Oh." Merry listened. Then she said, "When they get back . . . sure. Just tell her I called? Thanks."

Meredith turned to Mallory. "She's not home."

"Not home yet or not home?"

"She's out with her brother. . . ."

"Out . . ."

"Their dog ran away. But he always comes back."

"Not tonight," Mallory said.

Merry tried to stop herself from looking at Mallory, fearful of what she would see twisting in her twin's eyes. But she could feel Mally's thoughts hammering at her mind like fists.

NO TAKE BACKS

NO TAKE BACKS

The twins went to church on Sunday as usual.

It was Campbell's morning to sleep in. She was a Presbyterian, and Tim a Catholic. Since she'd had to give her girls and boy to the Catholic Church, she at least made their father take them to church while she luxuriated on the weekends of her two weeks off.

In the hall before Mass, they met Sunny.

Sunny had clearly been crying.

"You didn't find your dog," Merry said. "Poor baby. Pippen is such a sweetie."

"He was my birthday present," Sunny said, the tears starting fresh. "He was my seventh-birthday present. I can't stand thinking someone else has him."

Someone else doesn't, Mally thought, but said, "He could come back! You know those stories about dogs following their owners all the way across the country if they get lost!"

"She's right!" Merry said, impulsively holding out her arms. Sunny hugged her. Mallory didn't normally join in such dribble, but felt so sorry for Sunny she couldn't resist.

Mass was quick during Lent. Tim announced they were heading to his mom's for waffles. The girls relaxed in bliss. Grandma Gwenny's waffles were clouds of cinnamon and powdered sugar. They could forget dead dogs and sad old ladies.

But Grandma looked as sleep-deprived as they did.

"What's wrong, Ma?" Tim asked immediately. "Is Dad sick?" The Brynn brothers and sisters were close, even the sister who didn't live in the area anymore, but out in Portland. Tim talked to his brothers and sisters almost daily—if only to shoot them an e-mail—and saw his parents at least once a week.

"We're fine," Gwenny sighed, hugging Adam and fixing her eyes on Merry and Mally. "What's up with you two?"

"Nothing," the girls said together, and tried weakly to laugh.

"It's important to be careful," Gwenny said. "I mean it. This isn't a joke."

"Mom!" Tim cried, thinking for a horrible moment, with all the recent talk about puberty and womanhood, that Gwenny was talking about birth control. "They're not even thirteen and a half!"

"Hush, Tim. The girls are fine physically. They know what I mean."

Mallory longed to ask Grandma more specific questions. She wished Dad would quit yakking to his mother and leave—at least leave the room. Meredith hoped he'd say even more meaningless things. Then Grandma wouldn't say another word about any of it, they could go home and it . . . just wouldn't happen anymore. Her fingers itched for her cell phone. She wanted to call . . . anyone.

Gwenny turned on her heel, and they all followed her slim, straight back into her big country kitchen in the ranch-style house where they'd moved after Tim and Campbell had the twins. The table was set and the batter ready to pour. Grandma had made chamomile tea. Tim devoured his waffle and sat back to relax.

"Honey," she said to Tim. "Your dad's out back."

Tim grabbed another waffle. If he didn't run every night on the treadmill in the basement, Mally thought, he'd weigh four hundred pounds.

"How's cheerleading?" Gwenny asked Merry, as she watched Tim cross the yard and slap his father on the back.

"Well, after the big meet yesterday . . . it's going to be nothing," Merry answered. "We won. You know that. Did Dad call you?" Gwenny nodded. "We don't cheer for, like, baseball or golf."

"How's soccer?" Grandma Gwenny asked Mallory.

"I'm doing good. Not as good as I should be."

"How's swimming?" Grandma asked Adam.

"I hate the butterfly, but I'm the only guy who can do it, so they make me."

"Give you great shoulders someday. Your dad did the butterfly. Regional champion."

"Yeah," Adam said, diving into his waffles and sausage. "He shows us the pictures all the time."

"Want to watch TV, Adam?" Grandma asked.

"Okay," Adam answered, mystified. None of the parents and grandparents treated TV as anything but the last refuge. Grandma carried Adam's waffles to the den on a tray and then came back to join the girls.

"You girls want to learn to knit?" Grandma asked the twins.

The twins looked at each other.

Gwenny rummaged in the closet and dragged out a giant wicker hamper. She began picking through her yarn. When Tim and his father clattered in at the back door, Gwenny suggested, "Why don't you two boys take Adam and get some lunch? I'm going to teach the girls a little craft."

From the other room Adam said, "I just ate four waffles!"

"You're growing," Gwenny told Adam. She gave her husband a meaningful look—one he recognized from long association. Soon, he and Tim were backing the car out of the driveway with Adam in the back.

Of course, nobody ever unwound the skeins of yarn. Gwenny did demonstrate how to use the needles to cast on stitches, just so as not to lie on a Sunday. Months later, she did use those first stitches to make long, looped scarves for each girl, green for Merry and navy blue for Mallory. As Gwenny wound the yarn around her fingers and began to slide it onto the continuous round needle, Mallory asked, "Do you know about our dreams?"

Gwenny put the yarn aside and nodded.

Mally went on, "You don't see what they are, but about being separate, you know that. And how it hurts us? Do you think there's a reason? A reason why I see what will happen, and she knows that it did happen?"

"I'm sure! Why is that useful?" Merry chimed in.

"David Jellico . . ." Mallory interrupted. She paused before she went on. "He's not how he seems."

Their grandmother listened.

"She's crazy," Merry insisted. "She thinks David is some psycho wacko creep who sets fires and kills animals." Grandma Gwenny said nothing. "*She* thinks that. I don't! I don't have any proof." Grandma Gwenny still didn't speak. "And I don't want proof! Grandma, how can you go along with this junk?"

"It's not junk," said Mallory.

"It's only since the fire that you went loony tunes," Merry said. "Okay, if you think David is up to something, what do you want to do about it? What would you do if you could?"

"I'd see where he goes," Mallory said, after a long moment.

"How?"

"I don't know that. Grandma, would you do that?"

Grandma Gwenny shrugged and shook her head.

"I guess I could use my bike. . . ." Mally began.

"I guess I couldn't. I don't ride a bike anymore," Merry said. "She does, to humiliate me! I gave mine to Adam a year ago, and even then I hardly ever used it."

"I think we should find a way to follow him. Maybe not physically. A phone tree or something," Mallory continued. "That would mean telling people, though. Outsiders. But Mom says where there's a will, there's a way. I think we should."

Merry asked, "Do you promise to shut up when we find out David's only a softhearted guy who plays practical jokes?"

"Do you promise to shut up if we find out he's a freakazoid

who likes to kill animals and set fires?" Mally shot back.

"Maybe it's better just to ask questions quietly than take big actions, and not get others involved," Gwenny said.

Mally stirred impatiently. "I can be . . . what's the word?" she asked. "Subtle. I can be subtle. I can listen more than talk. I used to be good at that. Now, I seem to be all over the place with my mouth."

"You probably feel confused. We all act differently when we're confused and frightened."

"I'm never subtle," Merry said.

Even Mallory had to smile. "But you're always random."

After they kissed their grandmother good-bye, both realized that Grandma Gwenny had said only two sentences about their problem during the whole hour they'd spent at her house. And still, in her silence, Mallory believed she gave them tacit permission for what they began to call Operation David Detective.

At first, it was almost a joke.

For the first time in their lives, the twins set out to prove each other wrong.

Pippen the dog never did return.

After days and days passed, Sunny gave up.

"I hope it was a nice family who took him," she told Mally, taping a picture of her little border collie inside her locker with a yellow ribbon tied above it. A cold pebble of misery settled in Mallory's belly. It was the dog she had seen, as if through a curtain of fog, in her dream. She expected to feel triumphant, but instead was miserable when she motioned Meredith away from the group of girls crowded around Sunday's locker. She pinched Merry's arm, and whispered, "Don't you feel terrible now? Still think it was my imagination?"

"Quit being such a jerk!" Merry whispered back, pulling her arm away. "How can you talk about it that way at a time like this? Dogs run away all the time. Why do you have to make a big crime drama out of it and try to get some poor guy involved?"

It's Merry's friends who really love drama, Mallory thought with an inward sneer. *Especially somebody else's.* She watched them as they fluttered away for second bell. They all wanted to be the first to say, "I am so totally sorry. . . ." They would throw themselves around, remembering their own sad losses of doggies and kitties, crying big, fat tears until someone started comforting them. They looked like the twins' great-aunt Thea at the wake of one of their ancient cousins.

"Wakes," said Uncle Henry, Thea's husband. "They're like the World Series to her." Aunt Thea even went to funerals of people she wasn't related to. She came from out of state for them.

That day after school, Mally visited Grandma Gwenny on her own. She took her run late in the day, all the way to Gwenny's, a five-mile jigsaw of roads from her own house.

Her grandmother was delighted—but not, Mally quickly realized, entirely surprised when her granddaughter showed up. After she showered and got into one of Gwenny's old tracksuits, she said, "I hate fighting with my sister. This dream thing was already between us. Now the David thing is between us."

"Maybe you could pray about it," Gwenny answered. "I don't

like bothering the Lord with human problems. But I think saints like conversation. They used to be human. They probably remember making mistakes. I favor Saint Anthony, the patron of lost things, because I'm always losing something. But for visionaries, like you, you can't beat Saint Bridget of Sweden."

Mally was shocked.

Unlike Aunt Thea and some of her other Catholic relatives, Grandma Gwenny didn't go in for a lot of religious stuff. Gwenny was an action person. She had always referred to the Massenger women (her maiden name was Massenger) as "sturdy"—women who could pitch tents and clean their own fish. Thea, she always said, was the eldest of her four sisters and two brothers, but also the runt of the litter. She finished lacing up her Reeboks.

"You ready to go home?" she asked.

"Not really," Mallory told her. Grandma reached out for Mallory and held her close in a tight hug. "I'm not ready. For anything."

"That's why I suggested that you pray. Pray to feel it," Gwenny said. "It could work."

"Do you think Merry and I are the runts of the litter, like Thea?"

"I think that you are anything but. I think you are the warriors of the tribe, don't you? Like Saint Joan."

"I don't want to be," Mally said, pulling herself away from her grandmother finally and looking deep into her eyes. "Would you want to be?"

"No," said Grandma Gwenny. "But it isn't a choice you get to make."

That night as Merry was putting on her thirty-five kinds of face goop, Mally blurted out, "Okay, prove me wrong. Let's watch him. Let's watch where he goes."

"Mallory, no. I don't want to fight about this anymore. It's asking me to believe you can see the future before it happens. Which is already impossible. But even if I believed you, and I don't, if a person we've known all our lives did such a horrible thing, he wouldn't do it every day," Merry said.

In fact, she was showing more bravado than she really felt. Merry did believe in Mallory's vision, more than she wanted Mallory to know. She hoped she was hiding it well enough.

"Just one night, then," Mally said. "Just this Saturday."

"You're out of your mind! That's such a really great idea! We'll both wear ski masks and I'll get Crystal's dad's motorcycle! Whee! No one will notice!" Merry snapped.

She had a point. Thirteen-year-olds were dependent on someone else for every move they made. Even if David had a chip in his head that let them see his every move, how were they supposed to follow him?

Briskly, Merry said, "Mally, you have to stop this. First of all, it's disgusting and scary. Second of all, this is David we're talking about, who is no more twisted than you or Kim. And third of all, what if David *was* the dog killer of Ridgeline? What would we do? Have Dad drive us around? Or Drew? Until we finally saw a dog murder?"

It was a problem.

"I really wouldn't start riding around after him on my bike," Mally said. "I'm not an idiot."

"Then what?"

"Well, to start, you have to tell Kim about your crush," Mally said suddenly. "That's it. She already sort of knows. If you do, we'll get some idea where he spends his time and who with."

"Uh, that would be a negative. I'm so sorry. I have to go back to earth now, Mal. I've never told her in so many words." Merry thought back to the discomfort of seeing David sock Kim when Merry dreamed about his "garden." She didn't want to provoke anything else.

But Mallory begged.

"Please? For me? If I'm wrong I'll never bring it up again. I'll do your dishes for a month. I'll make both our beds for a month."

"She'll tell him," Merry said through clenched teeth.

"Say she can't. Just get her to tell you where he's going, so you can sort of casually show up there. Tell her you'll know by seeing him with someone else if he really loves another girl. Tell her you want a chance to talk to David."

"She's going to know that's shady. I would never do that."

"No, she won't." *Not if she's anything like you,* Mallory thought, before she caught herself. Even locked out of each other's dreams, they could still clearly hear each other's thoughts.

"Kim isn't stupid," Meredith snapped.

"I don't think she's stupid."

"You just did! I know you did. You thought that!"

"Mer, let's work together, please. I want to be wrong. I don't want you spending every Saturday night sleeping over at a house where there's a house-burning pet murderer."

"That's all fine. But it's impossible."

"So prove it. Help me figure it out."

"One night."

"Just one night."

"Promise me you'll stop this then."

I can't, Mallory thought, but knew that Meredith didn't hear her. "I promise, promise, promise."

The next day at early lunch, feeling like a fifth grader passing notes, Meredith pulled Kim out of the lunchroom. She'd first spent ten minutes in the washroom, rubbing her eyes with her fists and filling them with eyedrops until she looked distraught—or at least more messed up than she would ever have allowed herself to look in front of anyone but Mallory, except maybe for Drew or her brother.

"I have to tell you," she said, grabbing Kim's hand.

"What? What's wrong, Mer?" Kim was nothing if not drippingly compassionate. She was drippy *altogether*, Meredith admitted. Mallory was right.

But she was a good kind of drippy, she reminded herself. Mallory might be right, but Merry was loyal.

"I . . . I love David," Merry said, sounding, she realized, ever so slightly psychotic.

"Aren't you . . . that's a big word, Mer."

"I've loved him all my life."

"Wow."

"Does he love Deirdre?"

"I don't know."

"See? This is what I can't stand."

"What about Will?"

"It's a completely different thing. And it's over." That much was true. "I know I can't be with David now, Kim. I just want to know if he is totally in love with someone else so I can try to get over him. You don't understand. I knew you wouldn't."

"Mer, I do! But I can't just ask him. He'd tell me to stuff it."

"If I could see them together, I would know. Is that too much to ask?" Meredith burst into real tears—of fury, at her sister, who she could hear, clearly, enjoying this. Kim put her arms around Meredith. *Huggy wuggies again*, Merry heard her twin say.

"Oh, poor baby! Listen . . . David is so not in love with her. She goes to Queen of Peace, and he always dates girls from other schools so he doesn't have to see them after he gets bored with them after about a month!"

"But Deirdre goes to Memorial," Merry said.

"Not anymore. She used to until her parents found out it was the second leading school in the area for underage drinking."

"It is?" Merry asked, so honestly surprised that she quit crying.

"Yeah," said Kim. "Half the kids are down every weekend."

"Wow, that sucks. Are you sure?"

"Yeah, but about David . . ."

"Oh, yes!" Merry said, attempting to jump-start her tears but unable to pull it off. "So he only dates girls from Queen of Peace?"

"And even other places. Deptford Consolidated," Kim said.

"He just plays the field. That much?"

"I think girls get too serious for him too fast. Like, I overheard him fighting with Deirdre last week in the family room and she called him an effing crud."

"Because he was hooking up with someone else?"

"I don't know. But I bet it was."

"Kim, here's the thing. Just once, I want to see them together and then talk to him alone."

"Why? You're in eighth grade."

"So was Juliet." That was inspired, Merry thought!

"They didn't have eighth grade then. And plus, she was a year older, and plus, you only lived to be about forty then."

"Look, I think he feels the same way about me."

"Mer, I think David really likes you like a little sister."

"No, it's more. And if it isn't, if I see him with someone he loves, and have a chance to talk to him, alone, just once, I'll forget about it. Not at your house. I just have to tell him."

"Well, I know where he buries those poor, sad animals now. And I know he brings flowers."

"You do?" Meredith asked, her flesh tightening, as it did when she narrowly missed falling or spraining an ankle at practice.

"Well, he told me he buried Sunny Scavo's dog. I just asked him where and he told me. I had to walk away this morning because I knew and I didn't want her to see my face. Did you even know she was missing before today? She got hit by a car, the poor thing, and David found her. And he doesn't want Sunny to know. He wants her to think some nice people found her and she has a new home. He's like that."

"Where is . . . it?"

"What?" Kim asked. She had popped open her cell and was

reading a text. "Christian Allen is coming on to Caitlin. God! Caitlin is so hot. She can get a sophomore?"

"The place he buries those poor animals."

"It's up in the hills off Canada Road."

The Brynn family camp was off a dirt path at the end of Canada Road, about a mile up into the hills near Crying Woman Ridge. About to slather a french fry with mustard (a habit that nauseated even her father, who put M&M's in his popcorn), Mally felt Meredith's shoulders tighten. A chill spread from Mally's fingers up her arm into her belly. She thought she might throw up. She put down the french fry and held her water bottle to her forehead.

Caitlin Andersen, sitting across from Mallory, asked, "Cramps?"

Mally said, "Yeah. Hate it."

"Work out. Helps."

"I do."

"Reverse crunches. Want a Motrin?"

Mally said, "Sure."

Across the room, Merry was slumped against the cold concrete wall, with its coating of baby-poop green paint. Spots bobbed in front of her eyes like small squids. She clearly saw David spading up dirt, kicking the furry white-and-black bundle into the hole, but gently . . . *I mean, who would want to touch a dead dog?* Kim was telling the truth. But burying a poor, dead dog didn't mean you killed it! *He choked it. He hanged it,* she heard her sister think. *Mally,* Merry thought. *Laybite. Leave me alone!* She slid down the wall until she was sitting on the floor, her round-toed lavender suede boot wavering in front of her eyes. Her mouth went dry.

"Can I have some of your water, Kim?" Kim detached the Nalgene bottle clipped to the bottom of her backpack and thrust it into Merry's hands. For an instant, sounds of the screams and clinks from the lunchroom ramped up to deafening; then the world went black, as if someone had switched off the lights in a theater. She sat on the floor, with Kim crouched next to her, her arms around her knees. Sweat ran cold down both sides of Merry's neck.

"Mer! Mer! What's wrong, Mer?"

"Cramps," Merry said.

"Oh. Do you need anything?"

"No. I'll be fine. It's the first day is all."

"Look, you are totally upset about this. I'll find out where he's going this weekend. Okay? Can you stay over Saturday?"

"Absolutely," Merry said. She inched her way back up the wall, still unsure of her balance. Then she hugged Kim. "You are the best, best friend always." But in fact, she wanted to scrub herself hard in a hot shower.

She let go before Kim did.

SICK SENSE
SICK SENSE

"All it proves," Meredith began that night as they lay awake in the dark, "is what we already know. That he's a soft-hearted guy."

"What if that was true?" Mally asked. "Wouldn't this still be kind of a morbid hobby?"

"You could look at it like that. Maybe he wants to be a doctor. Or a vet."

"Maybe he wants to be an undertaker. Admit it, Mer. It gave you the creeps. Tell me exactly what you saw."

"No." Meredith didn't want to talk about Canada Road. Next thing, Mallory would have them hiking up there to dig up every dead cat in Cole County.

"Just tell me. Tell me what you saw when Kim was talking. What did she say? I felt how it hit you. You almost passed out, like I did."

"She just said that about the dog. That Sunday Scavo's dog got hit by a car. And then I saw him burying the dog. Very nicely! Not like a monster."

"Is there a nice way? You think?"

"Come on," Merry pleaded.

"Wait," Mallory whispered, gnawing the inside of her cheek, a habit Campbell constantly told her would end up giving her mouth cancer. "You saw David and the dog . . . but it had already happened."

"And?"

"I saw David before it happened."

"So?"

"MEREDITH! It's obvious. I see things before. I saw the fire before. I saw the dog before."

"You think seeing things is like *wee-ooo wee-ooo*? Come on. When I was little, I used to be able to think about where the Easter eggs were. I believed everybody could. . . ."

"No, no! That was little. Now it's big. And the thing about it is, we both see, but you see it after and I see it before. And you see what's all *nice* and I see what's . . . not nice. You saw the cemetery, so you think David is just a nice guy who buries poor road-killed pets. You saw him bury the dog, after the dog was dead. I saw the . . . the death, before it happened. And sure, I used to have little thoughts about little stuff, too. And I used to think everybody could. But everybody couldn't."

"And then it stopped, Mal."

"Why did it stop?"

"I don't know. I never thought about it."

"Do you ever think about anything?" Mallory asked.

"Shut your fat mouth. Actually, I didn't like it. It was fun when I was really little, but then . . . Mallory, I don't really remember, but I think I got tired of knowing what my Christmas presents were. I wanted to believe in Santa Claus. It was a drag to know so much. It stopped when I told Mom about it. Right before I got lost in the woods."

"So you put it out of your mind. Like the fire."

"I guess. I quit trying."

"So it used to be a thing you had to try to do," Mallory said.

"Wasn't it for you?"

"Yeah. Was hearing me ever anything you had to try to do?"

"No. That isn't like seeing something outside us."

"That's just being us. But why did seeing other stuff go away for *me?* I never told Mom about it. I guess I didn't like it, either. It wasn't like me thinking your math test for you. . . ."

"Or you being unable to punctuate a simple sentence without me thinking it for you. . . ."

"It was that I didn't feel like the other kids."

"I felt . . ."

"Like . . . old."

"Me too," Merry said.

"Like an adult," Mally continued. "I hated it. Even knowing I was getting an Easy-Bake Oven. Or that a card from Great-Grandpa was coming with a five-dollar bill in it. This is bigger, and I hate it more."

"Look, Mallory, don't go off. You're not sure this is all that big. Kim saw David *save* cats' lives lots of times. Stray cats that got hurt."

"Cats have nine lives! They get better! Who knows why they got . . . messed up? What if precious David was the one who tortured them in the first place?" Mallory hissed.

"You are so nuts."

"You are so dim."

It was a variation of the same thing they had been saying to each other all their lives. Neither of them loved the other less for it.

"Okay, listen," Merry finally told her twin. "I'm staying at Kim's Saturday. If he leaves, I'll . . . I'll call you and you can come and follow him."

"Okay. How?"

"Ride your bike," Meredith advised her, with a sneer she was glad Mally couldn't see.

"It's March, Meredith! I said even I'm not such a fruitcake that I ride my bike in the dark on slippery roads! And even though you like to make me sound like I'm six years old, I hardly ever use my bike anymore except for exercise."

"Bull. You ride it to school. You did last year."

"Once!" Mallory snapped.

"No, it was at least five times."

"Well, I'm not afraid to sweat. I don't know how you can be a cheerleader, because you have to sweat, Meredith. Why don't you have your sweat glands removed so you can be sure you'll never smell?" Mallory asked.

"Get Drew to drive you," Meredith suggested then.

"How can I do that?"

"Uh. Well, okay. Tell him you like David." Mallory made gagging sounds.

"I'd rather have my tongue cut," Mally said.

"You made *me*," Meredith went on.

"You do like David. Plus, Drew and I are going to a movie. With some of my four hundred free passes that Aunt Kate gave me."

"Like a date?" Meredith was dumbstruck.

"Like with Eden and her sister, Raina, and whoever else can fit into Drew's car. We're going to the *Star Wars* marathon."

"Well, so bring your cell."

"It starts at four o'clock. What am I going to do, jump up at nine o'clock if David leaves the house and convince Drew to run out of the theater and follow him?"

"If he leaves, I'll text you ODD."

"ODD?"

"Operation David Detective."

"Oh, please. Can you *be* more fifth grade? Why not just 'David left the house'?"

"Because Kim might see it, duh. ODD looks like a text word but it isn't. Do you have a better idea?"

Well, Merry wasn't that dumb.

Mallory didn't have a better idea.

She *would* have to tell Drew she liked David Jellico. The very notion made her want to curl up and sleep until Tuesday. But spying on him had been her big hairy idea. Merry wasn't responsible.

Mally sighed. "Okay," she said.

Through the interminable passage of what was, for everyone else, an ordinary Wednesday, Thursday, and Friday, Mallory gave herself over to the full-time hell of ceaseless anxiety. She went to bed at seven o'clock, the minute her homework was finished, expecting—almost hoping—David would do something crazy that would not force her to involve Drew at all.

Instead, she dreamed of Eden Cardinal. She dreamed of Eden kissing the man with the woodsy clothes. She saw them together. She saw the white mountain lion.

She woke up and couldn't stop mulling over Eden Cardinal.

Eden had come into the store one evening earlier that week when Mallory was watching the counter for her father while he drove Adam to swim practice.

"I have to get new cleats and I hate to," Eden said. "I know I'll outgrow them. I'm going to end up with feet the size of somebody in the NBA. They're already a nine and a half."

Mallory helped Eden find shoes that were thirty percent off. On an impulse, she said, "Drew Vaughan and I are going to the *Star Wars* marathon. Know anyone who'd like to go?"

Eden said she would love to go, adding that her sister, Raina, could drive her. A couple of her cousins and maybe her brother would come, too.

But why did she all of a sudden agree to go out with Mallory and Drew? Right now, when Mallory was in trouble? Was that paranoid thinking? After all, she'd never asked Eden to do anything with her. Still, it was weird for a high-school girl to agree to do something with a kid—even if Drew was someone Eden knew.

Maybe Eden would have agreed to go to the movies with Mally even before the talk they'd had that day after practice. Or maybe Eden sensed something about Mallory. Maybe she was some kind of freak like Mallory. That thought pestered Mally like a persistent mosquito. For what if Eden *was* some kind of freak, like Mallory? Say that was why she told Mally that "not much was strange" to her. If Eden was, maybe she knew why.

Maybe she could tell Mally what she saw. Or heard.

Was it pictures or voices for her? When and how often?

If Mally could just tell somebody other than Grandma Gwenny, who was so sweet but sort of closed off about all of it, she knew she would feel better. All she wanted was to be her normal, lazy, competitive self, the girl who loved sloppy clothes and World Cup and wanted to grow up and be Mia Hamm. Sports, in fact, were all Mally could tolerate anymore on TV.

She couldn't even watch *General Hospital*. She couldn't sit still long enough. Even her old movies now seemed like documentaries, since her own life had become as bizarre as sci-fi. *General Hospital* was skim milk. All people did was stand around for a whole hour, talking and talking and talking, about whether somebody's baby was really his baby or his brother's baby. It was so dumb she couldn't comprehend how she once loved it so much.

Mally decided that she would never again spend a sunny Saturday afternoon watching ten YourTimed *General Hospital*s or *Days of Our Lives* in a row. She made a vow. If she was wrong about David, she would never think of Luke and Laura or Bo and Hope or Stefano DiMera ever again. Never. Or Lucky. Or Patch. Never.

She would become a nun.

If it would go away, this seeing thing, she would give up TV forever . . . until summer.

. . .

At dinner on Friday night, Mally couldn't force herself to eat firsts, much less her usual seconds. Campbell zoomed in on this like a bird of prey in about four seconds.

"I cooked this pork roast," she complained. "I stood here and cooked this. I cooked this asparagus on a day off when I could have read a novel and gone to Power Weights with Luanne and Bonnie. The least you can do is eat it."

"I hate pork," Mallory said.

"You do not hate pork. You ate half a pound of bacon last week," Campbell said.

"I hate pork, also," Adam said helpfully.

"Shut up," Mallory snapped at him.

"Apologize!" Tim and Adam said simultaneously.

"Okay, fine. Sorry, you little copycat jerk," Mallory said murderously.

"Mom!" Adam whined.

"I said sorry!" Mally repeated.

"Accept her lousy apology, Adam," Merry told him. You could practically see the faint halo around Merry's head. Mallory curled her lip at Merry, but sideways—out of her mother's line of vision.

"I read it makes you stupid," Adam pointed out.

"PORK ROAST?" Mallory cried.

"That's why Jewish people don't eat it," Adam said.

"Jews don't eat pork because in the Bible—" Mally began.

"You said 'Jew!'" Adam shouted.

"What's wrong with saying 'Jew'? Dane Greenberg is a Jew," Mallory said. "Your friend Shaina Werner is a Jew."

"You say 'Jew-ISH,' " Adam said.

"What does that mean, *like* a Jew? Are we Catholic-ish?" Mallory asked.

"He thinks it's like a swear," said Merry. "Adam, honey, it's not considered bad to say someone is a Jew if you say it nicely. Mally, he's ten years old!"

"Eleven in a month!" Adam crowed. Tim ran his hand over Adam's blond buzz.

"I can't believe you're already going to be eleven. Tim, we should adopt a baby," said Campbell. "You're all growing up too fast. Mallory, you just eat your roast."

"No."

"Then leave the table."

"Gladly," Mallory said, knocking over her chair, then picking it up in a hurry when she caught her mother's unmistakable one-second-from-grounding glance.

"*Shabbat Shalom!*" Adam called after her as she ran up to her room and fell onto her bed. A moment later, unable to shake the jitters, she got up and threw on her sweats to go for a jog, though she'd run three miles that morning.

But she was no more than eight or nine blocks from home when she saw David Jellico, slowly passing in his dad's minivan. Just as Mally was about to dive into the bushes, he winked at her, and Mally forced herself to give him a big smile. Then she turned and ran for home, as if rabid pit bulls were chasing her. If she got kicked out of soccer, she'd do track, she thought, finally crawling up her front steps, with side-stabbing pain, afraid she was about to puke up her stomach full of nothing.

There was a note on the door.

The rest of the family had gone to the Belles Artes to see some movie with German subtitles. Merry was clearly trying out for Most Favorite Twin, or else Campbell had promised to go to the mall on the way.

The sink was also very clearly filled with dirty dishes Mally knew were intended for her.

She scrubbed the roasting pan and loaded the dishwasher.

Then she jumped into the shower, but barely had rinsed the shampoo out of her hair when she jumped out again. Grabbing her chenille robe, she sat down on the bed, convinced that someone was watching her.

Watching her?

There was only one tree close to their window, and its branches were as bare as bones on an X-ray. No one was sitting in the tree, or, when she looked down carefully, standing under it. The corners of Drew's garage next door were clearly visible, no one behind them. Mally sat down again. Gently, the branches waved in a brisk little breeze. Mallory watched them sway and sway. *David was making out with Deirdre Bradshaw. It was a heavy make-out session: He had his shirt off and she was kissing his shoulders. He reached up and ran his fingers through Deirdre's blond hair and when he began massaging her back, Mallory saw David twist Deirdre's long cashmere scarf in his hand. Deirdre started to push him away. David grabbed her hair.*

"Deirdre!" Mallory screamed in the empty house and fell back, the world dissolving with a silent whir.

Mallory had no idea how long she lay on her bed. But when she sat up, her legs were on the floor. She was almost kneeling. It was so dark she had to Braille her way to the door and the lights. The thought of the entire first floor, a sea of shadows, the only light a dim glow in the kitchen from the streetlamp five houses down . . .

For the first time in her life, Mally was afraid in her own house.

She put on winter pajamas and thick socks and tiptoed down the stairs. Taking a deep breath, she darted to the front door and locked it and each of the downstairs windows. No one in Ridgeline locked their doors—only old people at Crest Haven or big shots in the mansions at Haven Hills Golf Course. Tim's friend Eric Krueger, a cop, said that unless you happened to have windows that were slits in the ceiling, security systems were only useful for alerting the police where to find your body. If they were coming in, Eric said, they were coming in. Burglars didn't look for houses with people in them. That was the *last* thing they wanted. Mally peeked out the window over the sink. Next door, the Vaughans' basement lights were out, so Drew wasn't home with his friends. The only thing on was the little hall lamp Mrs. Vaughan always left burning when they went someplace. Damn it! But the light at the Johannsens', across the street, was on. Mallory could see the aquarium blue of the TV behind their sheer curtains.

Go to sleep, Mallory told herself. *Everyone'll be home in an hour.*

But what if they went to the nine o'clock?

What if they went for ice cream first?

They would never take Adam to the nine o'clock.

What if they dropped Adam off at Aunt Kate and Uncle Kevin's first?

She wanted to call Grandma, but remembered Grandma telling her that she and Merry were warriors, a pair of warriors. Massenger women were made of stern stuff.

And this was nonsense.

Back upstairs, Mally took two Tylenol PM's and ate a handful of Nilla wafers with a cup of Drowsy tea. The combination would knock her out within minutes, she hoped.

When it didn't, Mallory tried to add another element of boredom. She began her Algebra II homework. She hated all math, but it was satisfying to be able to do it. She'd have only two courses in math to take in high school to complete her requirement—while she was convinced that Meredith still did her multiplication on her fingers. But she finished all of the problems within twenty minutes.

Now what? Desperate, she dove under Merry's bed, a sure trove of trash magazines with skinny singers on the covers. She read all about Lindsey's feud with Natalie, and Ashley's feud with Tammie. Another ten minutes by the clock. Finally, she lay awake, her teeny reading light with its five-square-inch pool of light like a candle at her bedside. She listened to every click and snap in the old house, to the mice skittering across the attic floor, the bats rustling above the mice. Tim was always going to do something about them, but Campbell liked bats. Over it all, she heard the soughing of the wind in the big Celebration maple tree. What was wrong with her? She thought she should pray to Saint Bridget, as her grandmother had suggested. But wasn't Saint Therese better for protecting children? At thirteen, was she still a child? Saint Anne? Would Saint Anne look down and see a thirteen-year-old not-even-pregnant girl and think she had just tuned in to the wrong station?

Holy Saint Bridget, protect me, your daughter who sees and wants only to help, Mally prayed. *I don't even know why I'm afraid for myself, when I should only be afraid for Deirdre. I am afraid that whoever is after Deirdre might be after me, too. At least, he might be eventually. If you are there, protect me, so that I may serve. I want to be of service, but you can't if you're dead. Although you are dead and you're of service. I didn't mean it that way. Please don't be offended. I don't want to get off on the wrong foot. Amen.*

Mallory gave up praying.

She went over to full-time worrying.

The Scavos' poor dog was one thing, but what she had seen tonight was truly . . . way around the bend. It was the beginning of a rape. A rape? Maybe a murder. She should call Eden, no matter what Eden thought of her. Eden was older. She got it instantly when Mally saw the woodsy guy who was her crush. Or she should tell Campbell everything, even if it meant that her mother took her to a therapist?

Someone's life could be in danger.

A girl's *life.*

But in danger only based on the whacked-out wide-awake dreams of a crazy person who probably had posttraumatic stress disorder.

How could God let this kind of picture be shown to a thirteen-year-old kid who couldn't do anything about it? And how did she know for sure it hadn't happened yet? *I can't figure this out,*

Mallory thought, on the very edge of tears, *and figuring out is what I do.*

Why didn't her parents come home? Mallory wished, again, she could fall asleep. She knew that the active ingredient in the Tylenol was Benadryl. Could you overdose on Benadryl? Should she take more?

She fought to think about something else.

What was wrong with her? She was no sissy, afraid of the dark.

This house had stood for eighty-seven years. Brynns had lived in this house for eighty-seven years. She thought of all her great-grandparents, one of whom, Walker Brynn, was still alive in Florida. She thought of her great-greats before him and tried to pull all of them around her like a puffy quilt.

It didn't do the trick. She put out her hand for her phone to call Grandma Gwenny, but then, suddenly, the Tylenol PM kicked in.

Just as she fell asleep, Mally heard a sharp, loud pounding on the front door.

Three short, sharp knocks.

Oh, thank you, she thought. That was Meredith's signal, but why didn't her dad just come in? And she couldn't hear Meredith's thoughts, not even in the muddy way she could when Meredith was thinking about Will or splits or toe jumps. Though she would rather have pulled her own teeth than answer the door, Mally made herself wake up.

She crept downstairs and stood on her toes to look through the peephole. No one was out there. *Merry,* she cried with her mind. As she turned to go back upstairs, she noticed it was sleeting now—a dark, punishing, sideways spit of frozen rain, the kind late March always brought before giving it up to spring.

And then the same sharp knocks came again, but this time on the back door.

What would happen next? A gigantic blast? Was this going to be some horrible instant replay of New Year's Eve that would *actually* kill her this time?

Had she locked the back door?

No.

No one used it. As Campbell said, they preferred to wear out her only thing of value, an Oriental carpet runner in the front foyer. Mallory grabbed the kitchen phone, dropped to the floor, and dialed 911.

"Please," she whispered to the woman who answered. "I'm home alone and someone is knocking on all the doors and scaring me."

"Are the doors locked?" the dispatcher asked. "Is this Mally Brynn? Or Merry?"

"Yes. No. I don't know. I mean, I know I'm Mallory, but I don't know about the back door."

"Mally, it's Rita Andersen, Caitlin's mom. We're sending a car to check things out right now, but you go lock that door. Okay?"

"I'm too afraid."

"You have to, honey. I'll stay on the phone with you." Mallory crawled to the door and straightened up enough to flip the deadbolt. Did the knob quiver as she flipped the lock? Did it *turn*? Was that the pressure of another person's hand she felt on the other side when she tried the door to make sure it was locked?

"Please, Mrs. Andersen," Mally whispered. "Make them come quick."

"Where are your folks, Mallory?"

"At the Belles Artes."

"You give me your mother's pager number now. . . ." But as Mallory began to repeat the numbers, there came a huge bang on the front door, as if someone had used a mallet instead of a fist—three short, sharp blows, each louder than the next. "Mally, I heard that. Stay on the line. Thirteen, what's your ten-twenty? Possible two-eleven . . . sole occupant at one-one-three Pilgrim Street is a thirteen-year-old girl. You're okay, Mallory. They're a block away."

There was a full minute of silence. Then Mallory screamed as the knocking began again, fierce and sharp.

"Mallory? Mallory?" a man's voice shouted. "Look out the window. This is Denley Hames. It's Officer Hames, the school officer. Open the door, Mally."

Mallory threw open the door and leaped into Denley Hames's arms. "Someone was hitting the door! Someone was trying to break the door down!"

"Well, let's step inside, honey. This is Susan Moss. Do you know Officer Moss? She's the drug-and-alcohol teacher at the middle school now, for the fifth graders. May we come in, Mallory?"

"That could be a dent," Officer Moss said, pointing to a black mark on the pale blue door.

"It is," Mallory said. "But my brother made it when he rode his bike up the steps."

"What did it sound like?"

"At first, like knocking, then like someone was using a hammer to smash the door in."

"Let's take a look at the back," said Officer Hames. He unlocked the back door carefully, without stepping outside. "Lots and lots of footprints out here . . . if there was a roof over these stairs, we might be able to keep some of them from washing away. I'm still going to call for a photographer and a tech."

"What in the hell is going on?" Tim Brynn cried, bursting in the front door. "Mally, are you okay?"

"Daddy," Mallory cried, hugging Tim's waist. "Someone was trying to break in. Or scare me."

"Are you sure?"

Mallory was so shocked she let her arms drop. "Am I sure?"

"Every time we're away, something weird happens."

"Dad, do you think I'm lying?"

"No. But you've been having these spells. . . ." Tim said.

"Do you think I'm trying to get attention?"

"Of course not, Mallory! I just thought you might have been dreaming."

"Did you pass out, Mally?" Campbell asked.

I can never tell them, Mallory thought. *They would lock me up in my room forever. Or worse.*

"Mr. Brynn, someone was out there. There's mud on that back porch," said Officer Moss.

"There's mud all over those steps and half of the mud from Ridgeline on our kitchen floor," said Tim. "I have three kids who never heard of taking off their boots."

"Dad!" Merry scolded him. "You can see how scared she is."

"You *heard* me, didn't you?" Mally asked her sister. "It was . . . siow, Merry. Siow the worst."

"Yeah, I heard you! But I thought you were mad!"

"I was scared to death, Mer!"

"Who do you think it was?"

"The devil!" said Mallory.

"Talk sense, honey," Campbell said wearily. "All this drama! It had to be kids . . ."

It took two hours for the police to finish photographing, measuring, and dusting. Finally Denley Hames said, "It's not that it's just vandalism. Someone knew she was here. That's just not right." He added, "We're going to do our best to figure out what's going on here, just like we're still working on catching whoever was responsible for that fire. But I'd bet my redbone hound that the two things are related."

"Just don't put a yellow plastic tape up in front of my house," Tim Brynn pleaded. "My family's been through enough."

In bed that night, Merry whispered, "You don't think it was David."

"I don't think it *wasn't* him. I saw him driving around when I was running."

"So he bangs on the door? That makes no sense."

"Maybe he's mad about you knowing about the dog."

"Maybe."

"You admit I was right about the dog now."

"I semi-admit it. Or if I don't, at least I'm scared by tonight. Scared in my own way. Can you sleep?" Merry asked.

"I'm afraid to sleep. I'm afraid to dream. You don't know what it's like."

Merry decided that this wasn't the time to bring up her own dream about the old lady.

There had to be an upside to this. She asked, "Didn't you get any idea of who it was out there? Nothing? Not even if it was a girl or a guy?"

"No," Mallory said. She was still sitting up, shivering, despite the old quilt Campbell had draped around her shoulders. Campbell offered to camp out on the girls' floor, which Mallory would have loved, except that then she and Merry wouldn't have been able to talk. "That's what's so harsh about this. I didn't see it coming. Maybe . . . I'll tell you this. I don't ever want to sleep again. And I have to tell you what else I saw, before any of this happened, when I took a nap."

"What? You mean you saw something *else?*" Meredith asked slowly, dreading what Mallory would tell her. "You can tell me, Mally."

"I'm afraid to," Mally whispered, sliding down into her nest of quilts.

"Mal, you have to. If I'm going to believe this . . ." But she hadn't even finished her sentence when she saw that Mally had fallen asleep, fast asleep, while Meredith was talking.

It was Merry who lay awake until the sky behind the branches of the maple turned gray as a dove's breast.

BAITING THE TRAP

BAITING THE TRAP

It was after seven o'clock on Saturday night, and Mally rejoiced. Sitting in the darkened theater between Eden and Drew, she inwardly jumped up and down. Her sister hadn't called. She felt pure, total joy of having nothing happen.

She could have predicted that Merry wouldn't believe her about Deirdre Bradshaw. When Mallory finally got her alone, after the night of the knocking prowler, she told her about her blackout, about David and Deirdre. At least, Meredith *said* she didn't believe her twin. How she looked told a different story. *She doesn't want to believe me*, Mallory said to herself. *She's trying her best. I don't blame her. Put the dream with the door thing and it's definitely too spooky to handle.*

"You were just thinking about Deirdre because we were going to follow him," said Merry.

"I hope you're right," Mally told her. "I never hoped anything more." Now it seemed that she really had hallucinated the ghastly picture of David hurting the girl—and maybe the dog as well.

But only five minutes later, Mallory's phone vibrated.

Merry's text read *ODD*.

Mallory texted back, her fingers nimble in the dark. *Where?*

Within seconds, the phone trembled again. *Pizza Papa,* it read. *5 mins lev.*

"Drew," Mallory whispered. "I have to go."

"You're little. You can squeeze past."

"Not to the bathroom, you dip. I have to go, go, leave. It's an emergency."

"Come on, Mal," Drew huffed at her.

"I really have to go."

"Call your dad, then."

"I can't. They're at my aunt's."

"Call your grandmother."

"Please, Drewsky."

"No. All you do is have emergencies. Fires and midnight door-banging assaults . . ."

"I really have to leave! Now!"

Eden turned to Drew. "She means it. If you won't drive her, I will."

"Oh shit. Great. Fine," Drew said.

Everyone in the row behind shushed them.

As they drove, Mally kept consulting her cell phone. No word from Meredith.

"Can you stop at my house?" Mallory suddenly asked Drew.

"Want to drive to Softy's for a smoothie, too?"

"I just have to change."

"What?"

"I have to change clothes." Mallory hoped to forestall any griping he might do about this by making it sound private, like a girl thing. It apparently worked, because Drew shut up. Inside, she raced up the stairs and pulled on a pair of Merry's hip-hugging jeans and a couple of multicolored shirts, one longer and one sleeveless and V-necked. She threw open her sister's sorted-by-color makeup drawer and swept blush across her cheek, then nearly blinded herself whipping mascara onto her lashes.

When she jumped back into the car, she saw Drew's covert look of approval. "What's with this?" he asked. "You look like Merry. No, you look like you, but better. Why did you do it now?"

"Nothing of mine was clean," Mally lied, knowing it didn't explain the makeup. In fact, she didn't know why she had the urgent, sudden need to look like Merry, either. It had hit her between the ears like a command.

Finally they were outside the little strip mall that looped around the pizza joint.

Drew finally asked, "What's this all about? What are we doing? Do you want me to come in with you?"

"Yes," Mally said, then added, "No. Well, yes. I don't know."

"What's wrong, Mal?"

Dread clogging her voice, Mallory said, "I'm following David Jellico."

"What the hell for?"

"I . . . like him."

Drew gasped as though there wasn't enough room in the car for him to breathe. Then he studied Mallory's face in the light of passing cars. She was lying.

"You do not," he said. "You don't like him like a boyfriend."

"I do."

"Merry likes him. I've heard her say it twenty times."

"No, I do."

"Mallory, this isn't about you chasing a crush to the mall."

Mallory bit her thumbnail. She had never bitten her nails, and was surprised at how satisfying it was. "No, it isn't."

"What's it about?"

It was crazy, but she spilled the whole story: about the weird cemetery, and Sunday Scavo's dog, and the pounding. But she could not bring herself to mention Deirdre Bradshaw. It was too foul. When she finished, just as she expected, Drew stared at her like she'd picked her nose. Slowly he said, "I don't know Jellico. I think we have gym together. He doesn't hang with my friends. It would be completely sick to try to scare you by trying to break into the house. But why do you think he killed the Scavos' dog?"

"I don't know. Maybe he ran over it. I just think it's weird that he buries pets. Like his own and other people's."

"It's either he really likes animals or he's got a weird fixation."

"I didn't say he dissected them!" Mallory said.

"It's like being the dead-animal patrol. The guys from the city who come and scrape roadkill off the street. I was out there once when they came to get this big fat raccoon. The whole truck was filled with white plastic bags. I was like, boy, who do you have to know to get this job?"

"He did this before."

"He killed another dog?"

"No, he . . . he tried to scare us. We were sleeping over at Kim Jellico's for her birthday when we were little and he came mauing up the window with a stocking over his face."

"So he's a cat-burying, dog-burying dork and we're going out to see him at Pizza Papa's. And we got up and ran out of the *Star Wars* marathon for this. And you changed into Meredith's clothes. I'm sure this all makes complete sense. Does he have a dog with him? Did you get dressed up for the dog?"

"I don't even see his car," Mallory said, relaxing. "There probably wasn't any reason to come. Let's just wait five minutes."

She relaxed, laying her head on the headrest. Drew flicked on the radio and flicked off the headlights.

The tap at the window was so soft she almost missed it.

She opened her eyes.

David Jellico's face was next to hers behind the glass of the passenger-side window.

Mallory screamed. Then she sat up and smiled and calmly depressed the window button. "Hi," she said. "What are you doing? You scared the hell out of me."

"Getting some 'za. What are you doing?"

"Same. You know Drew Vaughan."

"Vaughan," David said, making it sound like a hello. "This is Deirdre."

Saliva gushed into Mallory's mouth. She tried to swallow. Deirdre was wearing a long cream-colored cashmere scarf with tassels.

"We were at the *Star Wars* marathon. Boring," said Drew. "If you've already seen them all."

"I'm not into it," David said. "Want to go look at the Ruby Slipper first?" he asked Deirdre.

"Or sit in the car and talk . . ." she said, all purry and sexy.

Mallory's brain screeched, *No!,* and she called out, "What, is something on sale at the Slipper?"

"All the boots," said Deirdre.

David looked at his watch. "It's only open another fifteen minutes, Merry."

Mallory shook her head sharply at Drew. He got the cue. He wouldn't correct the mistake and tell them which twin this really was.

"Can I come?" she asked.

Deirdre pouted a little. "Sure," she said.

With Drew standing outside the store rearranging the contents of his wallet, and David playing like he was Prince Charming putting the glass slippers on Deirdre's feet, they spent the next fifteen minutes in the shoe store. When it closed, David took Deirdre's arm and said, "We're going to grab a slice quick and go watch a movie at home. See you guys."

"We actually . . . came here to get pizza," Mally said. "Want to sit together?"

Because she had no money, Drew ended up buying pizza for

both of them, and asking for Mallory's to be wrapped up after she used a knife and fork to cut off two bites the size of a stamp.

All the while Mallory was panic-thinking. There had to be a way to keep him from taking Deirdre home to his house—or her house—alone. But what could it be?

"Why don't you go to the nine o'clock? You can make it," she suggested to David.

"We got a movie before at Video Box."

"What one?"

"Some chick flick," he said, as Deirdre punched him on the bicep. Mallory leaned over and punched him on the chest, but hard. His mouth fell open in a kind of shock, studying her. "You looked like Mallory for a minute," he said.

"I look like Mallory all the time."

"But she's always pissed off," said David.

"She is not. She's just, you know, aggressive," Mallory said. "She's a thinker. She's sort of a math genius." She realized how much she was bragging when Drew stomped on her foot.

"We should go, honey," said Deirdre.

"We should go, too, honey," Mallory said to Drew.

"Okay, sugar pie," Drew answered.

They walked out into the mall's tiny courtyard where merchants were drawing down the bars on their stores. "I'm going to run into the bathroom," Deirdre said.

"Me too," Mallory told Drew.

Deirdre drew a thick line around her perfect lips and began shading it in, the way Mally used to do with her coloring books.

"Deirdre," Mallory said.

"What?"

"David . . . he . . ."

"What?" Deirdre asked sharply, the last "t" like a bee sting.

"He's seeing another girl from Deptford."

"What?"

"He's seeing another girl from Deptford Consolidated. Andrea. Her name is Andrea," Mallory said, realizing, with a shock that made her sway so much she had to grab for the sink, that this was actually true. "For about two weeks. When he . . . said he had to go indoor golfing with his dad, he was with her."

"Meredith," Deirdre said. "Everyone in the universe knows you have this total obsession with David. Don't think that making up stories about another girl is going to come between us." She massaged a little golden peach cream blush into the apples of her cheeks, her fingertips stroking the color up toward the blond ringlets at her hairline.

"Except it's true. He has . . . he has her . . . he has her earrings in the glove box of his car. They're . . . silver half-moons."

"You are such a little snot. The cheerleaders at Memorial dread you coming. You are *not* going to be moved to varsity as a freshman. You can forget it. It's not junior high. It takes more than being a . . . dwarf to be on varsity there."

"She is not a dwarf!" Mallory cried.

"Who isn't?"

"Merry . . . I mean, I'm not! What, are you jealous? Not everybody can do what I do."

"Wiggle your butt and let people throw you over as if you were really a gymnast?"

"I am really a gymnast!"

"And your sister's a lesbian!"

"A what? And so what if she is? And she is not!" Mallory was shouting, her face hot.

"She dresses like a slob and she hates guys. Kim says."

"Kim says that about me?"

"No, about your sister, the super jockstrap."

"And what are you? You don't even know your guy is with somebody else. You probably have mouth warts, you slut."

"Toodles, Grumpy. Or is it Dopey?" Deirdre said.

Just outside, near the center doors of the mall, Drew squatted on his heels.

"Women," he said. There was nothing else he could think of. Jellico did give off some creepy vibes.

"You're not with Merry, are you?" David asked him. "She's, like, a kid."

"No. They're our next-door neighbors. She got all these tickets to go to the five-movie all-nighter. But she didn't feel good and we had to leave."

"She's hot and all."

"But like you said," Drew pointed out, slowly getting to his feet, noticing he was half a head taller than Jellico, "she's a kid. I've known them all my life."

"But I think sometimes, 'Wait until you're sixteen, little Merry.' She has the best ass. She's all over me. My sister . . ."

Then Kim and the real Meredith appeared, each carrying a go-cup from Latta Java, the only store still open.

Merry wore hip-hugger jeans and a green strappy T-shirt layered over a long-sleeved white one. If Drew hadn't noticed the colors of the shirts and checked to see that it was her right ear, not the left ear, that had a pierced earring, he would have thought she was Mally.

"Where's Deirdre?" David asked.

"I don't know," Kim said. "Dave, listen. Dad dropped us off but Mom and him are going to the nine o' clock. . . ."

"I know."

"So you have to give us a ride home . . . please?"

"I have plans," David said. "You guys were going to the multiplex with them, to another movie."

"But we wanted to check out the boots," Merry told him. "And now we're going to watch *Best Spring Break*."

"Or you could drive us just to the movies," Kim suggested.

"No, he can't," Merry said.

"Vaughan can take you home," David told Kim.

"I'll take you guys home," Drew said. Meredith elbowed Kim.

"David, I'm not supposed to ride with anyone but you," Kim reminded him. "No offense, Drew."

"Kim!" David griped, exasperated.

Deirdre Bradshaw burst out of the bathroom with Mallory at her heels.

"Let's go, David!" she cried.

"What the hell?" David gasped. "You little shit. You're not Meredith! What are you trying to pull?"

"Those are my good capris," Meredith said.

"You go. The mall is over," said the small man in a green uniform who had begun to clean. "The coffee has a door outside."

In the dark of the parking lot, the boys pressed the unlock buttons. Drew opened the doors of his Toyota and leaned on the roof. Jellico's face was so bloated and dark, it looked like he was about to seize.

"I asked you," he said to Mallory, getting down in her face. "What were you trying to pull? Why are you dressed like her? Why did you let me think you were her?"

Mally glared up at him. "None of your business. Get away from me."

"Leave her alone, Jellico," Drew said quietly.

"You're sick, both of you. Half people. You and her. Freak show."

"Shut your mouth, Jellico," Drew said again.

"You make me."

"Don't make me make you. I run cross-country, but don't let it fool you," Drew said, now so quietly his voice was barely audible to the girls standing on the fake cobbled walk.

"Drew, this is my fault. . . ." Mallory began.

"David, let's just go!" Deirdre said. David wheeled and stalked away, throwing the box of leftover pizza on the ground as he searched in his jacket pockets for his keys. As Merry and Kim piled into the backseat of David's Jeep, Deirdre stood with the passenger door open and tapped on the door of the glove box.

"Open this," she said.

"Why?"

"Why is it locked?"

"My iPod's in there. And my registration."

"Open it."

"Whatever," David said. He jerked open the door of the glove box. In it was his iPod, a few sheets of paper, and a hairbrush. "See?" he snapped, closing it. Deirdre grabbed his hand.

"Let me look," she said. She pulled out the envelopes and the operating manual for the car. Mallory saw a flash of silver. "She was right!" Deirdre screamed. "Whose earrings are these, David?"

"They're for you!"

"They're old, David! You got me old earrings? Antiques? What's her name, David? Is it . . . let me guess, is it Andrea? Was she afraid she'd get these caught on your sweater? Or on your belt buckle! You can go to hell, David!" Deirdre jumped out. With one stiletto heel, she kicked the door shut and began stabbing numbers into her phone. David jumped out after her, slamming the door on his side.

In the other car, Drew glanced at Mallory.

"I'm reliving my life here, Brynn. And it's showing me that almost every time I've ever been with you, including dragging a hose upstairs when you were five and I was eight to spray it out the second-story window, I got in trouble and it was your idea."

Too absorbed in the scene on the sidewalk, Mally didn't answer.

David was yelling at Deirdre now. Kim and Merry slipped out of David's car and into Drew's backseat.

"I'm asking you, Brynn," Drew went on. "I haven't been in a fight since I was in sixth grade. I was going to the movies for a nice, long night of vintage sci-fi. Now am I going to have to go drag that guy off her?"

"MY BROTHER!" Deirdre yelled. "My brother, who wrestles at Cornell and who'll kick your ass, you piece of dung!" David took a step toward Deirdre and Drew tensed, reaching for the door handle. But then David jumped into his own front seat and peeled out of the parking lot with a thin wail of tires.

"Maybe I won't have a sleepover," Kim whispered.

"You think?" Mallory asked with a snort.

"Stop it," Meredith told her. "Those are my best capris you have on."

"You always have your priorities straight, Mer," said her twin. "Don't you see that we got Deirdre away . . . ?"

"Laybite," Merry warned Mallory.

"Away? What are you talking about?" Kim asked.

Drew waited until a beefy guy pulled up in a big Dodge and put his arms around Deirdre, nodding at the others. Without a word, Drew drove Kim home. She hugged Merry and got out of the car, saying, "He totally has a temper, but I did not know he was seeing two girls at the same time!"

Drew shrugged. "Probably not the smartest move," he said, because he couldn't think of anything else to say.

They had begun to back out of the Jellicos' drive when Merry noticed that Mally's mouth had fallen open and her head slumped forward.

"Drew," she said slowly. "Mallory had a blackout. But she's fine. She had one a week ago from stress and they did blood tests and everything and she is fine. Let's just stop and get some ice water."

"Jesus!" Drew cried. "No way! I'm taking her to the ER!"

"Drew, listen," Meredith said. "I promise you. I love her even more than you do, and yeah, I know you love her. I would never hurt her. Just, look, she's already waking up. Just, please promise me one thing. Do whatever she says when she wakes up. Promise. Do whatever she says."

"Please, tell me what is happening. Or am I just the designated driver?"

"He's at . . . he's going to . . . it's okay. We can go home. I saw daylight. It was daylight, what I saw," Mallory whispered.

Drew got them all bottles of water. And though he kept asking the twins all the way home what had happened to Mallory, neither of them would answer.

Only one of them could.

A DATE WITH DRAGONS

O ne Sunday, Mallory woke up and felt funny. She announced she wasn't going to Mass. She told Tim she was sleep-deprived. It was two weeks after the night at Pizza Papa's. But the dream had not come back. Mallory believed something had happened that made David come to his senses on his own, and thank God for that.

Maybe she really was sleep-deprived. Maybe she had a cold. She got up and ate breakfast with her family (a bite of omelet, Campbell noticed, and one sausage) and went back to bed. She noticed how pale and worn out Merry looked, as well.

"You need to go back to sleep, too," she said.

"No way," Merry said. She didn't elaborate. Campbell left her alone.

"They're growing," Campbell told Tim.

As Mallory walked away, Campbell noticed a new roundness in her daughter's body. By the pencil marks on the door the previous week, Mally measured nearly four-eleven, as did Meredith. They'd grown almost an inch. "That's all it is. They're filling out and growing."

Tim was relieved. A female thing. Campbell would sort it out.

Monday was a Teacher Training Day. Mallory figured she could do all her homework then. But thinking about Merry made Mally toss and turn so much that her comforter and sheets were a mess after half an hour. Slob that she was, Mally couldn't sleep in a messy bed. Finally, she got up and slipped into her clothes, washed her face, and ran a brush through her hair.

Merry had stayed awake all night on Saturday.

She watched reruns of *The X-Files*. She watched *The Philadelphia Story*, which she had bought the previous summer from Mrs. Olin, but never watched, and which was probably made when her mom was her age. She watched yoga class at four a.m. and did all the poses. Finally, she fell asleep on the couch.

It was night. David was driving. The radio was blaring, and he tore off his coat. He slowed down when a girl Merry didn't recognize gave him a flirty over-the-shoulder glance. The girl kept walking, letting her hips swing a little. David slowed his father's van to a crawl. Fifty feet ahead, the girl didn't notice. Just as David bumped up over the curb, a bus came roaring out of a side street and pulled up at the stop. The girl got on. Merry could see David's face as she walked through the lighted aisle. His lips were drawn back, but not in a smile. David looked like a thing, a beast, like an angry dog. . . . Merry woke with a yelp of fear and ran up the stairs.

When Campbell woke, she had to step over Meredith, who was curled outside her parents' door in her big blue comforter. Merry clutched the comforter around her as though she was freezing, but Campbell could see tendrils around her forehead where sweat had curled her hair. *Even after so long, dreams of the fire,* Campbell thought. Well, it was enough to terrify anyone, coming that close to death. And then poor Mally, with the prank when they were out.

Somebody's kids deserved a good scare themselves.

When both girls were up, their mother suggested that they box up their winter clothes, and they did this without a bleat of protest and without, in Meredith's case, a wail of mourning that she had no clothes at *all* for spring. They folded the towels together. Campbell was beginning to think there was something seriously wrong.

Then Alli called and asked Merry to go to the mall.

Merry hesitated. If she didn't agree, Alli would think she was nuts. She covered the phone with one cupped hand.

"Come to the mall with me," she told Mallory.

"No way," Mallory replied.

"Please, Ster. I have reasons. I just, I don't want to go without you." Mallory looked Meredith over. Even after the fire, Merry had never looked so bleak and ghostly.

"I promised Mom I'd help her clean the camp cabins," Mally said.

"We'll be fine," Campbell called. "Go to the mall."

And so Merry agreed. She got back on the phone and told Alli that on the way to work, Tim would drop her off outside the north entrance . . . but with her sister.

"Mally hates shopping," Alli objected. "She'll moan and gripe the whole time."

"No, she needs new stuff. She needs new running shoes," Merry improvised.

"Oh . . . kay," Alli said, sounding unconvinced.

Merry hoped to be excited by the displays of summer clothes. But everything looked cheap and garish, even at Modernessa. She and Mallory waited patiently while Alli tried on pair after pair of white shorts, until she had two she couldn't choose between. She bought them both. They looked exactly alike except that one had a waist with a buckle.

"Do you want to go look for shoes now, Mallory?" Alli asked.

"No," Mallory said. "I don't need shoes. I'll just sit here and you guys go." Alli shot Meredith a disgusted look, as if to say, *See, what did I tell you?* Mallory actually did need new soccer shoes, since hers were beginning to pinch. But her dad would bring a ton of pairs home for her to try. And she could have them for cost.

Merry shrugged.

They all agreed on a pile of nachos the size of a Halloween pumpkin, smothered with jalapenos, cheese, and sour cream. And then Merry said, "You know, I think I'm getting a cold. Do you guys want to go home?"

"It's not even three o'clock," Alli gasped. Merry normally left the stores when the owners were lowering the metal grates over the doors. "Erica's coming to look at bathing suits."

"You stay. I'll call our dad," Mally told her.

But the Brynns' answering machine pointed out that they were away from the phone just then. Adam's voiced piped up, "*If we like you, we'll call back!*" She couldn't reach her father on his cell, and when she finally got Rick at the store, he told her that Adam and Tim were picking up some inventory in Deptford. They'd be back in an hour.

Merry called Grandma Gwenny before she remembered Gwenny would be with her sisters, as well as Campbell and her other daughters-in-law, getting the cabins ready for spring. Grandma and Grandpa started spending most weekends in the big cabin in April. There was no cell phone coverage up at the camp, and the phones in the houses were turned off in winter.

"We'll just have to wait until Dad closes the store," Merry finally said.

"Maybe Drew will come and get us. It's not like it's a huge ride."

"It's a twenty-minute ride, Mal."

"Yeah, but he feels sorry for me since he thinks I'm mentally ill," Mallory said.

Mallory punched in Drew's number. Drew groaned. He had to be at work at five. It was forty minutes to the mall and back. "I'll give you gas money," Mallory told him. "I'll give you more movie passes. I'll give you two. Otherwise, we'll have to just sit here. Come on." Reluctantly, Drew finally agreed. They were to meet him outside the bookstore in twenty minutes.

The twins went outside and lounged on the brick wall in front of the bookstore. It was a beautiful, languid day, the storm drains running with meltwater, a haze of green shimmering around the branches of the trees—not quite about to bud, but nearly.

At home, Campbell's daffodils were up, and the only ice left in the whole county was tucked under the recesses of the rocks up near the ridge.

Across the street from the mall, people were outside, rushing the season, taking down storm doors and ripping away plastic coverings. There would be more cold nights and cement skies. Ridgeline could always count on an April blizzard. But today, the air was too full of promise to keep it all outside. What felt cozy at Thanksgiving now felt cramped and stale. People wore sweaters but threw open the windows.

Mally was pumped because outdoor soccer practice would begin next week. It was going to be such a good summer.

She needed to think about that.

She was strong and uninjured. Coach promised her she could count on starting at midfield, the most important defender. Tim drilled her a couple of nights a week in the backyard. Mallory was teaching Adam, who was interested in soccer at last. Someday, she would coach his summer league.

And until yesterday, Merry seemed pretty good, too.

She was using her hand again in routines, back walkover after back walkover down the hall—doing her idiot practices to music in front of the mirror, smiling so wide that she looked like some kind of predatory creature instead of a happy girl. ("You have to make them see your teeth in the top row," she told Mallory, who said that little kids in the *first* row who saw that face would be scarred for life.)

"What happened last night?" Mallory finally asked her sister. *Oh, please Saint Bridget,* Mally prayed, *let her say, "Oh, nothing."*

But Merry turned to Mallory and said, "I had a dream."

Mally didn't have to ask about whom. "Anno," she said, patting Merry's back. "Was it awful?"

"He was stalking this girl. He was going to grab her. I could tell."

"What happened?"

"She got on a bus," Merry said. "I woke up."

"I thought it was over. I thought that nothing would happen ever again because it didn't happen. After I had my dream."

"But it did. David was driving the van. It was late at night. . . ."

"No, Merry, it was during the day. I saw that it was during the day. I saw just where it was and it wasn't on a street with a bus stop."

The day was beautiful. Merry wore her jean jacket but Mallory had on only a turtleneck under a short-sleeved T-shirt. The girls spontaneously huddled together in the apricot light of the afternoon sun.

"So what I saw, he already did," Merry said.

"And what I saw, he didn't do yet," Mally said. "I didn't even see David. I just saw a place and I knew something bad would happen."

"Maybe he didn't know it yet."

"Maybe. I don't know what the rules are!" Mallory cried. "I have to know the rules!" She brushed both her arms until the goose bumps lay down. "So, here. We'll do the same thing. It said Crest Haven. I saw a sign. That's the old people's condos. The tennis court. There was no ice. So it would have to be later, when all the ice was gone."

"Most of the ice is gone," Merry said.

"But it's still a little cold," Mallory begged her. "Isn't it a little cold?"

"Not much," Merry said softly. "How are you going to know?"

"I'll know," Mallory told her. "It was pretty specific. I saw a girl the other time. I saw Deirdre. Maybe I'll have another dream." She rubbed her arms again with both hands. "I don't want to have another dream. The truth is, I have no idea."

"But what do we . . . do it for the rest of our lives? Until school lets out? What if we stop him next time and then he does it again? We can't devote our whole lives to following around David Jellico. I can't even go see Kim. I'm too scared," Merry said urgently.

"I don't blame you. No, this time, we'll tell him."

"*Tell* him?"

"Tell him we know he's a sicko."

"Isn't he going to wonder why we know?" Merry asked.

"I frankly don't give if he wonders how we know. All that matters is that we can convince him."

"You think we'll be able to?"

"Yes! You saw him burying the dog. I saw him kill the poor thing. I know he was going to hurt Deirdre. Maybe rape Deirdre. You saw him chase that girl."

"If only there was some other way out of this."

"Think of one, then. Please. I don't want it. I can't! Otherwise, it *will* be the only thing we do for the rest of our lives," said Mallory. "Once he knows we know, he won't ever dare to try it again. It's the only way."

"Maybe, Mally, we could just go to that policewoman, the one who came here when you heard the banging on the door. And just tell her!"

"Tell her what? That I had a dream about a guy who didn't do something I thought he was going to do?"

Meredith sighed. "It was an idea."

"It will be daytime and we'll be together. We'll be okay."

"Ster," Meredith said. "I just can't handle this like you. I never thought of us thinking about stuff like this, Mally. We had it good, all our lives." Meredith kicked the warm stone with the heel of her shoes, considering how she'd hardly gotten started on her future before she had to consider the good old days.

And then Drew arrived, and though he'd really never looked at them normally since that night at the pizza place, today it was as though a clean rain had fallen on all their faces. Their neighbor was the old Drewsky—with ancient Van Halen CDs cranking and cheeseburger wrappers all over the floor of his car. Mally sat in front, and they played headbangers and she almost forgot how much had changed. They went through the drive-through and got supersize fries. Drew squirted ketchup on Mally's bare leg. She flicked it on his jeans.

Cleaning her hands off with a napkin, Mallory sighed in contentment and rolled the window down just halfway. Drew was about to complain about the noise of the wind when she saw the sign.

"Drew, stop," she said. "Back up a little."

"Now what?"

"I think I saw something. Yeah, I did! Look, Mer! My bike is back there! Remember I told you my bike was stolen out of the garage? That's it! We'll get out here and walk the rest of the way home. It's not even a mile. Look, back there, leaning against that garage that's just the frame?"

Merry screeched, "A mile? Your bike? Your bike is just . . ."

"We'll be great! I can ride her on the handlebars," Mallory rushed on.

"I have to take off," Drew said. "I'm already practically late."

Drew was a stocker at Bill's Star Market. He said lifting the crates of chicken stock and lettuce kept him buff and the few bucks he got each week kept him in gas. Mallory literally hauled Meredith out of the car and squeezed her elbow. They waved as Drew slowly drove off.

Finally when his old green Toyota turned out onto Cambridge Street, Merry cried, "Are you out of your mind? Why am I even asking? Your bike was never stolen! Why did you do this to me? This place is like a mud factory! Why are we here?"

Mallory could barely keep her teeth from clacking in the bright sunlight. She turned up the collar on her turtleneck.

"It's the new housing development," she said to her sister.

"Duh!" Meredith said, nearly stamping her foot with impatience.

"Well, when we passed, I noticed the sign," Mallory said.

Meredith looked up. They were standing under a green street marker.

It read "Crest Haven."

"You said it would be the old people's condos," Meredith whispered, her chin beginning to quiver. "I thought we could run in the back door of the old people's condos if he did anything. We don't know what's back there. There's nobody here. The houses aren't even finished. You don't even know if there's a tennis court. It's not that nice out yet. You said it would be."

"We'll just walk back there. I'm probably totally wrong."

"Why? Why, Mallory? Why do we have to do this? Why do we have to know this? What if you're totally not wrong?"

"Then we do what we said."

"Mal, I'm calling Dad."

"Don't."

"Why not?"

"Because whether I'm right or wrong, what are we going to tell him? Are we going to tell him this . . . whatever vision I see and you saw? Do you want him to know, Merry? What if we get David to stop this and then we see something else someday? What if . . . what if Dad thinks there's something wrong with us? I thought about all this. Didn't you?"

"No, I tried to ignore it. And what do you mean, us? This is all your idea."

"Ster," Mallory said. "You know I'm right."

"We could end up in therapy until we're sixteen."

"We could end up in a nut place, Mer. Or boarding school. I could tell that Dad just about had it when the banging thing happened."

"He can't blame you. That would be so totally unfair!"

"No, I don't mean it like that. I mean, he was starting to think that something about us . . . okay, about me, was weird. He was acting like I was going hysterical. I think there's stuff about Dad's family, about the women in his family, that we don't know."

"You *were* hysterical."

"No, I mean, like, nutso hysterical. If we just do this, maybe it's over forever. What if there was a reason we went through all that pain and the little kids were even almost hurt? To save somebody's life?"

"Let's just walk back there, then. I don't want to stand here forever. You're cleaning these shoes for me."

"I don't know why you wore platforms."

"I didn't know we were going hiking in the mud, hello."

Together, glancing left and right despite themselves, Mallory and Merry began to make their way back past the model home with its three gables and huge double bay windows, past the finished houses with their "For Sale" signs, to where the sidewalk ended and paving gave way to planks. The final cul-de-sac was invisible from the road, and only one house was under construction, the raw framing like a child's Tinker Toy building. The other lots had numbers and strings delineating houses that existed only in the dreams of young families.

"See, there's nothing here. Thank you, God," Merry said.

"What's that?" Mally pointed at a track that went back toward a tiny wooded area—almost the idea of a forest, like a model at a plant nursery. They saw that the pool had already been bucketed out, squared off, and that a contractor was readying the sides for eventual concrete surfacing.

And behind the pool, there was a wide area boundaried by chain-link fence.

The tennis courts must have been poured last summer, before

anything else, so that the huge machinery needed to roll out and divide two double courts would never have to go whomping through someone's future front yard.

Meredith reached for Mallory's hand.

Parked between the gates of the two separate courts was David Jellico's car.

"Okay, we're not going to think about this," Mally said. "Ster, if we think about it too long, I'm going to lose it and so are you, and, plus, even though we can't see anybody in that car doesn't mean there isn't anybody in it. And so I'm going to run this way. . . ."

"What do you mean, this way? I'm going where you're going."

"We're going to go around separate ways. I'll be able to see you the whole time. We're going to go around so we can come in on both sides. He'll look up and see me, and then I'll distract him, and then you'll yell and he'll see you. If he has anyone in there . . ."

"What if she's hurt?"

"I told you, we aren't going to think." Merry grabbed her hair, as Campbell did when she was worried. "Think, now. Think what Grandma said. If we weren't supposed to do something about it, I don't think I would have seen it in my mind pictures."

"What did he do? What is he going to do?"

"Like the dog, Mer."

"Oh, no! Oh, Mallory, I can't . . ." Meredith began to pant.

"Take off your shoes," Mally said.

"I can't stand in the mud!"

"It's okay. I can. I'll give you my running shoes."

"Then you'll have to stand in the mud!"

"I can. I don't care about it. Let's just do it." Meredith quickly laced up Mally's shoes. Impulsively, they hugged. Then Mally set off at a slow lope between two houses and disappeared into the small stand of birches and evergreens. Merry ran through what would be two backyards and behind what she guessed would be a locker room for the tennis players.

She heard them before she saw them.

"No!" the girl's voice came, muffled, through . . . through what? Merry stopped, stepping closer. She heard David's voice, pleading, then lower, almost a growl; and the girl's cry was sharper this time, accented, "I said no to you!" The green door to the locker room was half open. Meredith did not think that anything on earth would let her open it all the way. But when the girl cried out again—and Merry could tell from the noise that she was fighting, scuffling—she pulled the heavy door back so fast it slammed against the wall.

"What's that?" David called.

Meredith crept into the dim interior, past lockers, through a shower stall to what appeared to be some sort of bathroom, with mirrors and counters. A plaid blanket was spread in one corner. A girl's purse lay on the blanket. But the girl was on the tile floor, grabbing for her bra, struggling, pushing to get up. David was half on top of her, holding her down. She was pretty, little, a Latina girl not much bigger than Merry was. Her sweater was torn and her lip was bleeding. And in David's clenched fist was his belt.

"Who's there?" David yelled.

"Your worst nightmare, David," Merry said. She had no idea how or why she was able to make a sound anything stronger than a squeak. But she came off like Superwoman.

Sobbing, the girl grabbed her purse and ran past Meredith, out the door. She could hear her babbling, in Spanish.

"You psycho little shit," David said. He sat back, against a counter. "What do you think you saw?"

"Who is she?"

"Like I'd tell you."

"Tell me or I tell Kim. I tell Bonnie and your dad."

"Some little slut I picked up at the mall. She works at the freaking pretzel stand. Jesus, Meredith. She wanted to."

"She *so* looked like she wanted to," Merry said. David rose slowly to one knee. "Don't even think about coming near me. I'll scream and every construction worker out there will hear me."

"There's no one out there," David said slowly, smiling, as if he wanted to soothe her, quiet her with soft words, as someone might do with an excited animal. "It's Sunday."

Meredith turned and ran back through the shower. When David's hand grazed her back, she forced herself to turn and nail him in the jaw with the heel of one of the platform sandals she carried. Blood pooled in bright red stitches along the cut, and David's hand went up involuntarily. Meredith didn't wait. She sprinted for the door. She was past his car when he caught up with her again, finally grabbing the back of her sweater and yanking her down into the mud.

"You're not telling anyone anything," David snarled. "Ever."

"Don't hurt her," Mallory said then.

David looked up, keen as an animal, his frustration nearly a scent in the air. Mally wasn't out of breath and looked as calm as she would have looked coming in from her run. "Get up, Merry," she said.

Merry pulled away from David and ran to stand next to her sister. Under the wide sky, with the sounds of traffic less than a block away, she felt safer. But David was slowly making his way forward. *Serpentine,* thought Merry. It was a vocabulary word. The blue eyes she thought were so beautiful were opaque, expressionless as water. David's blond hair was flat with mud and sweat. He was unfolding himself toward them, not quite creeping, not quite walking.

"No closer," Mallory said, pointing at David what looked to Merry like a big silver drill. "David, this is a nail gun. My dad used one when he built the store building. I was only ten but he let me use it. I know how. It's not hard."

"Bullshit," David said, creeping forward.

Mallory's knees literally began to shake, as they did after a hard game. "David, no! Don't! I found it on the floor of one of those houses out there. I'm telling you the truth! There are nails in it. Big roofing nails." She saw David measure the distance between them. Mally used her right hand to grab her left and stop her shaking. He could run toward her, but if she told him about the nails, maybe he wouldn't move until they could leave. "If I shot this, it would really mess up your face. I would really shoot you in the face. I would, I really mean it. I won't let you touch my sister. You're wrecking your whole life, David! You didn't do anything really bad yet. You can go to a doctor or something. Think of your mom, David!" Mallory began to cry. "David, maybe you're not really bad. Maybe you're sick."

David stopped. He stood, half crouched. Mallory could feel his readiness to leap at her if she tripped or dropped the nail gun.

Still pointing it at him, Mally felt Meredith pull at the waistband of her jeans. They backed up, opening a bigger space between David and them.

"You have to leave," Mally said, her tears and her leaking nose coating her face. "You have to. Merry already called our dad, David. You might be able to grab me, but you can't grab both of us. Lots of people know we're here. Drew Vaughan knows! He dropped us off." The girls kept backing up and David still crouched on the ground. The closer she got to the road, the braver Mallory felt.

The phone rang, but stopped before Merry could answer. She opened it and punched in her father's store. The line was busy, but she whispered to Mally that they really could dial 911 if they had to. It was safer if they could call Drew. Less likely to cause a big fuss for their parents and everyone else. Mallory didn't want Kim or Bonnie to know this had ever happened. She wished she could forget it had happened.

They made their way back through the sucking mud, step by step. Mally wasn't sad or even completely terrified anymore, but she couldn't stop crying. She called, "David, this is your last chance! To just get in your car and leave. You sick piece of garbage! You almost killed my little brother and my cousins. You burned Merry's hand. You tried to scare me to death. It's over now, David." Mallory held the nail gun in her hands, her arms extended. "Merry, try the store again. If no one answers, call the police. Will you admit it, David? Will you tell the police that you tried to burn us up? How could you do such a thing to us? I should shoot you anyhow. Maybe I will if you don't go right now!"

With a look so purely evil it nearly knocked Mally breathless, David turned and loped toward his car, jumping in and cranking the engine. He shot past them, splattering the two of them with icy mud as he careened past.

Mally dropped the nail gun and sat down hard on the ground. Too wobbly to stand, Meredith plopped down next to her.

"He's gone. He's really gone," she said. "Soso. Don't cry. He doesn't know if we really will tell. He'll never do anything again, Mal. Never." Mallory couldn't stop crying. She wiped her face with her shirt. For the only time in their lives to that point, Merry was the one who kept her head. She didn't shed one tear.

"I thought I would have to shoot him with the nail gun," Mally sobbed. "And the nail gun didn't really have any nails! It runs on air and I couldn't pump it up. He could have . . . he could have run over both of us, Merry!"

"But it was worth it. I saw the poor girl he had in there. She ran by me."

"What'll he do?"

"He didn't get to do anything but hit her," Merry said. "He was ripping off her clothes."

"He won't try it again. You're right," Mally said. She got up to her knees and wiped her nose and eyes again with her sleeves.

"That's so gross."

"I so care. Do you have tissues?"

"No, but . . ."

"Well then, stop it. I just, God, Merry. Before you believed in this, I did. I sort of lived with it longer than you did. I feel like I'm cracking up!"

"I know," Merry said. "I'm sorry." Merry turned to look out at the road. "What about when he's older, Mally?"

"Mer, we're, well, we're children," Mallory said, her eyes opening wider and fresh tears spilling over. "We can't guard the world from David Jellico. I think he's scared. But if he does anything else, adults will have to take care of it."

At the same moment, they heard the sound of a car, stuck and grinding to get out of the mud.

Mallory gripped Meredith's shoulder. But fear was quicksand. Neither girl was able to move. The earth might swallow them. At last, choking, Mallory said, "Merry, he is going to try to run us down. Come on! We have to get behind something!"

"I can't," Merry screamed. She threw herself on the ground, trying to curl herself into a ball.

"Get up! Get up! We have to run straight back, to where there are houses with people. Behind the housing development. Right now, Merry!"

They heard the car rev its engine and begin to slip and slice through the mud.

With Mallory pulling her, Merry stumbled to her feet. The sound of the car was louder, then even louder, the horn bleating, so near, almost upon them. *But he won't be able to follow us through the tennis courts,* Meredith thought, running with all her strength. *He'll have to go around. We just need to get back to the tennis courts, less than half a block.* And by the time David made the detour, they would be in those backyards they saw, so far away.

They finally heard the yell.

Drew was shouting, "Stop! It's me!" at the top of his voice. The girls spun around in disbelief. The green beast of his ramshackle Toyota truck was barely visible under the mud. David had zoomed through the muck like a madman off-roading.

"I never saw anything so beautiful," Meredith whispered. Mallory put her hands over her face. Drew swung up and out of the driver's seat and approached them. Mallory leaned her head against his chest. When Drew reached up and stroked her hair, she didn't stop him. Mallory felt so little. The top of her head barely hit his collarbone. Drew picked up the nail gun.

"Were you going to nail somebody, Brynn?" he asked.

"Yes. But it's empty," she admitted. "I'm glad he didn't know it."

"Jellico." It wasn't a question, so Mally didn't answer it. Instead, she said, "We're going to get the seats dirty."

"I can wash the seats. Let me get a blanket out of the trunk," he said, his voice breaking. "Just a little trip to the mall, huh? And your bike was stolen?"

"We couldn't tell you. We still can't," Mallory said, biting back tears. "You won't want to be our friend."

"Too late," Drew said. "I was born into it. Now, I'll take you home so you can get your clothes in the washer before you tell me what this really is all about."

"We can't," Mallory said, pulling the blanket around her. The sun winked out, and the wind stiffened. Ragged gray clouds seemed to strain overhead, as if winter had forgotten something and was hurrying back to get it.

"Why did you come in here? What happened to work?" Merry asked, for once the stronger, the less depleted of the two.

"I called in sick because Merry didn't answer her cell. I figured if Merry didn't answer her cell, she had to be dead," Drew told them.

"Drewsky, you really don't want to know," Mally said as they turned out of the housing development, back toward Pilgrim Court and home.

"I really don't, but I think I have to," he said.

"You'll be sorry," said Meredith. "We are."

THE LONELIEST PLACE

For a long time, neither of them would feel quite safe without the other in sight. When they heard parents talking about how much kids changed when they turned thirteen, they had to bite their lips to keep from falling into a frenzy of laughter. They both felt cored out, their whole former souls replaced by other beings.

"All I want," Merry said one day as she was painting her toenails, "is to feel exactly like I felt before. I don't need a boyfriend. I don't need to make varsity. I just want to feel exactly like I did before."

"I'm becoming a nun," Mallory said. "I'll be the only one who isn't seventy-five. I'll be, like, the beautiful nun, and people will say, why is she here? What tragedy was in her life? I'm going to be Sister Genesius. He was the patron of actors. I spent all those hours watching soaps!"

Campbell heard them laughing behind their door and was

relieved. Although she couldn't figure out why both girls spent so much time at home—doing things like reading! Playing cards and trivia games! Playing *Monopoly* with their *brother*!—she felt as though she had not heard them laugh for months. When she overheard Mallory, in passing, tell Adam, "I love you," she nearly wept.

They were healing, she told Tim.

Tim didn't mind. Mally was available to help out at the store more often. Merry actually volunteered to babysit Adam, though he insisted that she refer to it as "hanging out" with him. The girls went to school. They went home. They practiced what they did well. Merry went to cheerleading every night until six. Mally began her practices for summer soccer. They listened to music and slept.

There wasn't one always missing and one always nagging to be driven to this girl's house or that girl's house or the new shopping center only thirty miles away, and could they pick up Kim and Erica on the way?

Tim was stretched out on the leather sofa in the den late one evening when he noticed Mally slip into the room and sit down beside him. He made room for her by swinging his feet over the back. They watched the Stanley Cup playoff game together. They hadn't done that since Mallory was eight years old.

The girls didn't mind the period of restfulness, either.

There were no dreams.

Merry told her friends that all the garbage with the fire and everything meant she had to really book for finals. Mallory told Eden, who called, worried, that she was just kicking back for a while. It had been a weird year.

One day, they went with Drew to Burger Heaven. He never got the true story the day he found them in Crest Haven. But later, what they told him was almost the truth. There was no point in trying to fool him. And there was no point in going further than they had to.

Mallory played with her soda straw until he took it away. Then she said, "Drew, whatever we say now never goes anywhere but here."

"I mean no matter what," Merry added. "No matter what you hear about us. You're our oldest friend. But if our parents or your parents find out . . ."

"They'll put you in a pretzel factory," Drew said.

"No doubt," Merry agreed.

Mallory began, "Identical twins, some identical twins, have what's called—"

"Telepathy," Drew said. "I always saw you do that. You would say you wanted a plum and she would come out of the house with a plum. Now tell me something I don't know."

"Well, that's the thing," Mally said, hoping for an easy fake, the thing she did so well on defense, that Drew would accept. "That's how we figured out that David wasn't okay. We talked back and forth in our minds about how weird David was, how he yelled at Deirdre, and about how he buried the Scavos' dog."

"Why did you talk in your minds?"

"We couldn't say it out loud. It was too freaky," Merry said.

"And none of that links up with him *killing* the dog or *hurting* Deirdre," Drew said.

Mallory took a deep breath. This was true-blue Drew.

"I dreamed that he was going to kill the dog," said Mallory.

"And I dreamed that he had," Merry said. "I saw him bury her. In my dream."

"You dreamed it?"

"Yes," Merry said.

Silence huddled around their booth—while all around them, the bursts of laughter from kids and teenagers, the clink of dropped silverware and shouts of the short-order cooks seemed to fade. Instinctively, Mallory moved closer to Meredith on the plump red plastic bench.

"Did anything like this ever happen to you guys before?" asked Drew.

"Not until just before the fire," said Meredith. "We don't know why it was then and we hope that it will never happen again."

"What did he do to that girl out there?"

Mally said, "He scared her. But I think he would have raped her." *He would have murdered her,* she thought, hearing Meredith think the same thing.

"I don't know how to take this," Drew said.

"Seriously," said Mallory. "We think David set the house on fire at our uncle's on New Year's Eve. We think he's the one who was banging on the door when I was home alone."

Drew raked his reddish hair. "It's like part of me wants to believe you, and part of me can't."

"If I told you we felt like that, too . . ." Mally said.

"Then I would believe you," Drew said. "Brynn, what are you going to do now?"

"Nothing. Sleep and not have dreams."

"Nothing since that night?"

"No," said Merry. "Except I dreamed about the girl we saw out there on a bus."

"Did you ever think about me telling him that I know?" Drew asked, making a sculpture on his plate with his fries, a house and, behind it, two rectangular squares. Tennis courts.

"That's great!" said Mally. "That is a great idea! Tell him you know. He's scared of you. You're big. You're our friend. You wouldn't be scared he'd cut your tires or anything?"

Drew lounged in the booth. "You're such a kid, Brynn. If he did cut my tires, do you think I'd have to think twice about who did it? And if he would have done anything really bad out there, they could have practically followed the trail of breadcrumbs to his house. Tire marks. Fingerprints. Hair and blood. He left everything but his name written down."

"I never thought of that," Merry said.

"That's why you have me."

They weren't sure when it was that Drew confronted David.

But one day, Kim pulled Merry aside and said, "I have a message from David for you." Merry's stomach turned to frost.

"What?"

"He says he's sorry he scared you that time. He was being weird. That's what he said."

"Okay."

"What did he do?"

Siow, Merry thought to her sister. And with Mallory's words in her mouth she said, "He should be sorry. He splashed me on purpose with mud when I was running. I didn't even know it was David. I just heard this car behind me and thought I was going to get run over!"

"Oh, that sucks," Kim said.

"Maybe all guys are idiots at his age. It made me get over liking him, though."

"Drew isn't an idiot," Kim answered.

"Drew's not a guy to us. He's our friend."

To Drew, they were grateful, forever, for their freedom. When the Brynns ran into David at the multiplex, he was with a group of guys and merely smiled briefly at Tim before slipping into another line to buy tickets. He looked away when Mallory stared at him, his jaw flushed.

The girls no longer saw David cruising when they ran. He seemed as eager to avoid them as they were to avoid him. They ran together in the mornings now—Merry moving the ritual of choosing her clothes to the night before. Each day, they pushed themselves a little farther up toward Crying Woman Ridge.

Their legs grew chiseled.

Mallory soared down the field.

Merry's tumbling was spectacular. Cheerleading tryouts for high school were only a month away.

Merry knew that Kim couldn't understand why she didn't hang out after practice as she had last year. And it wasn't easy for Meredith to go home on the beautiful long spring nights after practice. But she had a strange sense of the world holding its breath, as if what seemed to have ended would come with a final symphonic note, a final clap of thunder after a rain shower. After a taste of adulthood, which she imagined as a daily confrontation with life-changing choices, she felt safer being a little kid.

Kim asked her, "Is it because of how David acted? He's acting so freaky. He's barely speaking to me, Merry. Is that why you don't hang out?"

"It's not, Kim. That was my fault," she said, the words sour in her mouth. "I had this little-girl crush and it wrecked his relationship. That's not why I'm not hanging out."

"Then why? I mean, I completely understand you not wanting to be at my house, but you don't do anything!" Kim said. "Everyone asks. Caitlin and Erika and Crystal and Alli, everyone."

Meredith pretended to be ashamed. She finally lied, confiding that she was grounded until the end of school, except for cheering practice.

"I told you about studying. Well, my grades were crap. If I'm going to try out in the fall, I had to raise them to be eligible. And of course, my perfect sister got nearly straight A's."

Merry made Kim promise not to tell, and recognized sadly as she did that telling Kim to keep a secret was a guarantee that she wouldn't have to explain it to anyone else.

Sadly, also, she told Will Brent, who now seemed terribly sweet and safe to her, the same thing. She had to work on her grades. She goofed off too much. High school was coming. They would both meet other people. He was puzzled and hurt. Merry thought, *This is so great. I really like him. We're so lucky we can see the future and the past.*

She wished the school year would wind up fast. The second semester had been the longest two or three years of her life.

Although she looked forward to high-school tryouts, there was a veil over even that. She wasn't a tough girl. She wasn't the kind who went looking for trouble. Why, she thought—as Mally had months before—did she have to be this bizarre way? One night, as she was reading—God! She, Meredith Brynn, was reading a novel her *mother* had given her, and because she didn't feel like doing anything else!—Merry realized that she and Mally had closed themselves into a cocoon.

It was much safer.

It was much lonelier.

She wondered if a point would come when they knew for sure that they could venture out.

The late April day of Mally's first game—at home—finally arrived.

Eden let the coach know she needed a family-related absence that day, which didn't go down too well. He told Mallory she would have to be at forward, so she sank deep into practicing shot drills. She thought of those who called her the Quitter. So on the nights when there was no formal practice, she spent hours passing and kicking in the backyard.

The night before, Tim worked with her until he gave in, saying Mally had worn him out. And Mally was bushed, too, and chilled, as though she were coming down with something. She woke every hour that Friday night, annoyed by the slow crawl of the red digital numbers of the clock. If she couldn't get some decent sleep, her reactions would be slow, her understanding of the scope of the field—Mally's best gift as a player—would be blurry. Finally, at four a.m., she got up in disgust, brushed her teeth, and sat in silence on the back porch, cross-legged, for hours, visualizing plays.

Just after seven, she made coffee for her dad.

"Jitters?" he asked. Mallory nodded. It was more than that, though. She hadn't dreamed, but something was nagging at her.

"You're ready, superstar," Tim said. "You own that field. It's your home turf."

"I know, Dad. Where's Merry?"

"Took off on her run already. She told you to hit 'em."

"*Merry* got up at seven o' clock to run?"

"Don't have a heart attack," Tim told her. "She wants to catch most of the game. She'll come later with Mom. Ready?"

"Ready," Mallory told him, but her body was disconnected from her head.

Adam climbed into the backseat of Tim's truck with its stencil of soccer balls on the side, lined up like dominoes.

Meanwhile, Merry was still running. She felt happy and strong, even though she was alone. Although her mother had offered the night before to come with her, Aunt Karin had called first thing in the morning, asking if she could possibly bring baby Timothy over to see if he had an ear infection or a virus. The poor kid had been up all night sobbing. All in all, Merry thought, it was just as well. She needed to finally accept that she was safe—anywhere in Ridgeline, her sleepy little town with its nightmares washed away.

When she got to the foot of the hill path, she had a strong desire to see if she could make it up past where she and Mally had turned back the day before. And so she began to climb up toward Crying Woman Ridge, up to the opening of Canada Road. Her legs wanted to quit on her. Her lungs wanted to quit on her. But it still felt good, pushing herself to the wall, thinking of Mally running nonstop for almost two straight hours at her game. Finally, she hit the top of the path. On impulse, though she'd already run two miles, some of it uphill, she turned and headed toward their family camp. A little fire road she'd never noticed looped away off "their" road, directly under the rocky shoulder of the ridge, and seemed a natural place to make her turn.

So, barely running now, Merry slowly gave herself over to the pleasure of thinking about how great it would feel to head down-hill. She nearly passed the odd, rectangular clearing at the back of the loop, where someone had cut and piled brush to make a clear space probably ten by sixteen feet wide. Stones were placed at regular intervals—some smaller mounds were encircled by little stones, larger ones marked by stones taken from the ridge, from the top where the ridge dropped away sharply to the Tipiskaw River that ran through the New York State hills surrounding Deptford and Ridgeline. From the Brynn camp, a long path veered back and forth to take walkers down to fish or swim. But the bigger kids— although they were routinely forbidden—loved to climb up and look over at the places where the sheer drop was sixty feet.

Merry stopped, lunged into a stretch, and stared at the stones.

When she realized what they were, her throat closed as though she were swallowing her own heart.

She turned to beat it back down the hill.

But David stepped out from behind the brush pile and said, "Hi, Merry. I know it's you, because I passed your sister, the Ter-minator, at Memorial Field on the way here." Paralyzed, Merry listened as David said, "So, you see, it's just you and me, Meredith. I knew that eventually the two of you would make it up here. And someday, it would be only one of you. Like when that bitch Mallory had a game. I can explain how you followed me up here and told me how depressed you were. I tried to stop you. I tried to grab you, but you were too fast for me." He made a sad clown face.

Meredith began to run, but she was tired and David gained on her in an instant. He grabbed her shirt and then her hair.

"My mother knows where I am," she said.

"So what?" David asked, letting go of her hair and then twisting her arm up behind her back until she cried out. "It'll all be over by the time she gets here."

"David, why?" Meredith pleaded. "Why?" She had to buy time. "You're not a bad boy. You can get better."

"Are you saying I'm sick?"

"David, you know you're sick!"

"You stupid cow. Remember how Mallory felt when she held that nail gun on me? I feel that way all the time."

"No, you don't!" Merry said. "You're sweet to Kim, and to your mom!"

"Only because I have to live with them," David said.

"So the girl at the tennis courts? She wasn't the first?"

"You don't need to know that. But, okay, what does it matter? She wasn't. Not by a long shot."

"None of them is . . ."

"Yes, one of them is! And no one knows where she's buried," David said cheerfully. "Or even who she is."

"Please let me go," Meredith said. "Please think of Kim! Kim loves you! You can't do this! Let me go. I won't tell. I didn't tell before, did I?"

"Not a chance," David said.

"Then let go of my arm so I can pray." She fell to her knees on the hard ground. "David, you're a Catholic, like us. Don't you know that—"

"Do you think I'm afraid of hell, little troll? I *am* hell," David said.

Meredith dropped her head on her hands. *Siow, Mal,* she whispered in her mind. *Siow, I'm afraid. I hurt.*

Across town, Mallory sneaked the shot into the net after the tall forward, Trevor Solwyn, faked a shot and passed to her. But Mallory didn't get up from her slide and do the happy dance.

Trevor, for weeks regretting her snarky comment, jogged to her side. "Mally? Mal?" Trevor said, and shook Mally's shoulder. Mallory's eyes were half closed, her lips pale. "Coach!" Trevor shouted. "Mally hit her head! I think she's knocked out!"

Tim was down four tiers of bleachers in four seconds, Adam scrambling behind him. Madison Kirkie's mother, a doctor, also jumped down onto the grass, all 180 pounds of her, and trotted over to where Mallory lay. In a row, like young deer, the two teams of leggy girls stood with their arms linked, silent with fear. But before Dr. Kirkie could get there, Mallory was awake, then quickly up on her knees, screaming, "Meredith! Meredith!"

When Tim got to her, she grabbed him with all her strength, almost ripping the sleeve from his windbreaker with the team logo from Domino Sporting Goods.

"Daddy!" she shouted, not caring who heard. "Daddy, we have to leave right now! We have to leave right now."

The coach said, "She needs to see a doctor, Tim. She conked herself a good one!"

"Mallory, settle down, honey. I'm going to take you in to urgent care. It's our second home now," Tim said. He had to drag Mallory toward the car as she protested.

"Be okay, Mally!" called Madison and Casey. Trevor bit her lip.

Mallory was already pleading with her father. "Dad, please! This is like the other time! At the cheerleading meet. I didn't hit my head, Dad! Meredith is in trouble! Please, Daddy, listen. Remember when we were little and she was lost in the woods? This is like that! Daddy, please!"

An electrical prickle ran along Tim's palms. "I'll call your mother," he said, and did. They spoke briefly. When he snapped the cell shut, he said, "Meredith should be back from her run any minute, and your mother thinks you may be having little seizures—"

"Daddy! Merry left *before* us! That was hours ago! Our run takes forty minutes. Call home. Call Merry's cell." Tim did, and listened to his own voice answer the home telephone. He was frightened then, unsure what to believe. Merry's cell rang and he heard her message: "Merry Brynn! Your turn!"

"She'd answer! She always answers! Always! You know Merry would rather cut her finger off than miss a phone call! Please listen," Mallory begged. "I'll go to the hospital. I'll have my brain scanned. I'll let you check me in. But first drive up to where we run, almost to the camp. Please, Daddy!" Tim hesitated. He would never forget the time that Mallory "talked" tiny Merry out of the woods.

But Campbell told him to meet her at the hospital. "Oh God!" Mallory screamed, throwing herself around in her seat belt like a chained animal. "Give me the phone, Dad! Give me the damn phone! At least that."

In shock, Tim handed Mallory the cell and backed slowly out of the parking lot.

She dialed Drew's home phone, getting a wrong number. "Shit!!" she cried, and Tim, about to shush her, stopped at the look on her face.

Mallory dialed again. No answer.

She couldn't remember Drew's cell.

Stop, she thought. Drew's cell. *Five oh nine . . . five oh eight. Yes!* But Drew's voice mail picked up. Sobbing, Mallory shouted, "It might already be too late! You have to go to our camp. Drew! Drew! Wake up!"

"Honey, that's enough," Tim said, and Mallory threw the telephone at him.

It was not prayer to God that Merry was repeating—although she did ask God to spare her life, or at least, if he could not, to spare her pain—but *Siow siow, Mallory! Mallory! Mallory! I'm hurt, hurt, hurt! Danger, danger, danger!* She could hear her sister's agitation. Mally heard her. Mally would come, but would it be soon enough?

"Get up!" David told her roughly. "You could've said the whole Mass by now."

"I was praying for you, David," Merry said. She didn't know if he heard her. His eyes were like identical pieces of marbled glass, and flecks of spit collected at the corners of his mouth.

"I'll give you one chance," he said. "Go ahead and run. Climb up those rocks, little cheerleader, and I'll count to twenty."

"Where?" Merry asked, stalling, stalling. *Mally! Mally!* she screamed in silence.

"You choose. It's your funeral," David said.

Meredith tried to pick out a path along the top of the ridge that she could run, as she'd run the balance beam when she was little. Slowly, she began to climb, five feet, six feet, David counting behind her. Another few inches. She gained the top and turned to face David.

"Ready or not, here I come!" he whooped. Merry took a deep breath. She did not need to look down at the jagged rocks that lined the riverbed. If she pushed David, she would still go over.

She gathered her determination and made her choice. *Mally*, she called once more, but gently. *Giggy.*

Then she drew herself up.

Just as David's hands gained the boulder an inch from her feet, Merry flung herself forward over David's head in a full front flip, landing on both knees, stones biting into her flesh. At once, she was up and running, already imagining the strong hand grabbing her collar, jerking her down. But instead, she heard David roar, "What the hell?"

Merry froze in mid-stride. Did she dare to look back? Would this be her last fraction of a second on earth?

Then she heard a scream—a scream so piercing that it barely sounded human—followed by the sound she would never be able to describe, the wet, heavy, impossibly grotesque thud.

She scrambled to the top of the ridge and looked down, horribly far down, then shut her eyes against the sight of David's leather jacket, his head, mottled with red . . .

"No!" Merry cried. She grabbed her own head and slid down the rocks, creeping past the graves, moaning and wondering how she would ever make it to the bottom.

At the opening of Canada Road, her legs gave out. And though she didn't know it, so did her consciousness.

It was the same woman Merry had seen before who bent over her and shook her head sadly, then reached out to reassure Merry. She was not old, after all. She had a young face, but with silvery hair, thick beautiful hair. Grandma Gwenny's hair was white when she was not much older than Campbell was now. The lady had not pushed David. No one had pushed David. Without words, the lady told Merry this was not her fault. Not her fault. Not her fault.

When Drew Vaughan found her, Merry was asleep, her face streaked with tears and dust, her head pillowed on her hands. She woke when he picked her up.

"David's down there, Drew," she said softly. "David fell off the ridge."

"Sweet Jesus. I'll call the cops," Drew said. "Let's get you down to the car first. Your knees are all swollen and cut up."

"I can't feel them," Merry said. "I'm sorry, Drew."

"I'm sorry, too," Drew said. "Bill fired me. I'm the Brynn Emergency Rescue Team of one." He settled Meredith in the car. "Before I call, what do I say? Do you want me to tell them he tried to hurt you? Did he try to hurt you? Did he do more than try?"

"I'm okay," Merry said. "Let me think. Tell them I was running and I heard him scream. Yeah. Then I climbed up there and stumbled on the way down because I was in a hurry to call you. That's all," Meredith said.

"Why wouldn't you have called the police first?"

"I'm only thirteen? I'm freaking out? I broke my cell phone? I'd have to really break it then, wouldn't I?" Merry asked weakly. She pulled her green slimline phone from her jersey pocket. "Good enough. It really is busted, anyhow. How did you know? Oh, sure. I know. Mallory called you."

"I felt my phone vibrate while I was stacking cans of tomato juice. I looked at the number. It was your dad's number."

"How do you know my dad's number?"

"Mally and you and him have numbers only one number off. 6886. 6885. 6884."

"What will I say to Kim?"

"Meredith, don't feel guilty. The fact that David caught you up here probably saved a girl's life. It's not your fault."

"That's what the lady said," Merry told Drew. "Something scared him when he was coming after me."

"Okay," Drew said. "I'm sure you know what that means. Please don't tell me."

Campbell was already at the hospital when Drew squealed into the lot with Merry. Mallory was pacing at the front door, dialing her sister's number over and over on Tim's phone. Without meaning to, she threw the phone down on the grass when she saw Drew's car and began to run. Merry was out before Mallory could put her hand on the passenger-side handle.

"Yes, it was!" Meredith said, in answer to a question nobody heard Mallory ask. "I'm fine. I'm okay. I think he's, Mal, I think . . ."

"He's dead. I know he's dead," Mallory said, reaching for Meredith's hand, pressing it to her own dirty, hot cheek.

Drew told the Brynns, "David Jellico fell off the ridge. The police are there. Merry called me."

"Meredith, my God!" Campbell cried, pulling her daughter close to her. "How did it happen?"

"I don't know. I was running, and I heard him fall!" Merry told her mother.

"Why didn't you call me? Why did you call Drew?" Tim demanded.

"I pushed the wrong button," Merry said, wiping her eyes and nose on her palm. She held out the phone.

"This phone is crushed," Tim said.

"I fell running down," Merry admitted.

Campbell and Tim stood locked in one spot, a hundred expressions of bewilderment rising to their lips and sinking like mist.

Then Campbell asked, "How do you know David is . . . hurt that badly?"

"He fell too far," Merry said.

"Oh, my poor Bonnie," Campbell said, closing her eyes. "I'm going to go."

"I want them to be looked at," said Tim. Adam clung to his father's arm, huge-eyed and stunned silent. "You're limping, Merry."

In the hospital that night for observation, Meredith and Mallory slept in the same room. Neither of them dreamed.

HEAR LIES

Hundreds of students lined up outside Lonergan's Funeral Home in Deptford before the doors opened—hours before the wake began. They waited in a line that snaked around the front of the building and nearly met to form a circle. There were girls holding each other up and sobbing, boys with hair combed flat instead of gelled up, standing stoic and pale beside their parents. Kids from Ridgeline Memorial and Deptford Consolidated. Families from St. Francis. Doctors from the hospital with their wives or husbands.

And every nurse within a radius of twenty miles.

Though David Jellico hadn't been the best-known kid at school, he'd been good-looking and successful, and had a core of a few loyal friends, mostly other golfers. But more than that drew the town and even the county out that night. The death of any young person was a subtraction of a disproportionately large part of the whole. Ridgeline's students came out together, with someone there from almost every one of three hundred families. But kids from surrounding schools were summoned by text and e-mail. Even David's picture in the *Reporter* that day was a portrait of poignancy. Everyone felt the assault was greater, and the ripple of empathy was wider than it could have been for any adult, however beloved.

Campbell barely came home for the first three days.

She was with Bonnie day and night.

Even Dave Senior, Kim and David's dad, could not bear the terrifying whipsaw of grief that battered Bonnie around the clock. But Campbell could. And only Campbell could induce her to take a sip of tea or a bite of toast, a fifteen-minute nap from which she woke shaking and wailing, crying out for Campbell to bring David to her. In Ridgeline, Bonnie was a beloved figure—much better-known to anyone who'd ever broken a leg or had an appendix removed than her professor husband, who taught economics at SUNY Hollendale. Since becoming a department head, Dave Senior often came home only on weekends. But Bonnie had been the Cub Scout den mother. She'd fund-raised for the cheerleaders' warm-up jackets and uniforms, treated the mounts' neck strains and the tumblers' bruises. Kim's house had been a sort of all-purpose clubhouse, not only for Merry but for a dozen other girls. Unlike Campbell, who made the twins and Adam walk a fairly narrow line, Bonnie was understanding and easygoing. When Caitlin Andersen was caught with a cigarette, Bonnie, not Caitlin's mom, Rita, administered the talk about wrinkles and skanky skin—and oh, yes, lung cancer and heart disease. And the talk stayed between Bonnie and Caitlin. But Rita knew, and blessed Bonnie for her influence.

She and most of the mothers and fathers who had kids at Ridgeline Junior High and Memorial felt they had a duty to Bonnie not only to comfort her but to mourn David ritually—for he could have been, so easily, one of their own daughters or sons. And Bonnie saw them, though only Dave could shake their hands. Bonnie was barely able to dress. Campbell helped her pull on stockings and a light blue wool dress. She sat clinging to Campbell—who had held Bonnie's hand when she gave birth to David, and later, to Kim; who had sweated with Bonnie and the surgeons over dozens of lives, old and young, grieved mightily when they lost, and felt like Olympians when they beat death back.

A surgeon never saw David.

The fire ambulance that drove down from Crying Woman Ridge after firefighters gently lifted him up from the riverbed proceeded swiftly through town with no lights or sirens.

Meredith had begged her parents to allow them to stay home. In grim silence, Mallory didn't even try—knowing it would be unendurable to Campbell to even suspect that her daughters would not want to comfort their oldest friend in her deepest misery. And so Meredith and Mallory dressed identically on purpose, so that no one but their parents could entirely prove which of them was which. In fawn-colored wide-legged pants and modest navy cardigans, they sat with Adam in a corner, on a triangular sofa, their hair drawn back in velvet scrunchies, trying to be as inconspicuous and expressionless as they were able to be. The long wide legs of the pants hid Merry's swollen knees. They let people think that the closeness of the two families kept them from praying at the kneeler near the closed coffin or gently touching the big boards of photos of David as a little football player, a junior golfer or, last summer, swimming in one of the natural pools of the river where he'd died, or patting his nine-iron, leaning against the wall.

In some of the early pictures, the Brynns were with the Jellicos, at July Fourth picnics, birthday parties. Merry could not stop staring out of the corners of her eyes at those pictures and the astonishing lie they told, which only she and Mallory would ever understand.

In the front row of baby-blue cushioned folding chairs, each wrapped in fabric skirts like seats at a wedding, Kim cradled David's brown leather jacket in her arms like a baby and wept constantly, surrounded by all the cheerleaders except Merry. Merry knew she must go, should go, but couldn't bring herself to take the twenty steps. Even a sharp look from Campbell couldn't convince her. She was sure that standing near the casket long enough to comfort Kim would make her truly, violently ill. Her few bites of dinner sat in her stomach like lumps of paste; she could feel her guts folding and rolling. She had not told even Mallory all of it— not the words David had said or the animal scowl on his face, not the blank spaces that were his eyes, the sound of his scream and of his fall, and Meredith's eerie, puzzling certainty that someone or something unseen had come between her and her death.

She finally knew for real how Mal had felt before—when all of it was to come, and all of it was hers alone to bear.

The chain that bound Merry to all this intolerable grief would never be broken. She couldn't bear knowing what David would have been, or what he might already have done. Mally might have done it better. Mally was built tougher. But telling Mally everything she didn't see wouldn't cut the chain in half between them. It would double the weight. She held Adam's hand and tried to think of the lyrics of songs.

When she saw her father approaching, her hands and feet went icy.

"You need to see Bonnie and Kim. And Dave. You need to, both of you. I'll stay with Adam," Tim said. "Imagine if it were one of you."

I did, Merry thought.

I can, Mally thought.

"If it were one of you—and last New Year's Eve, it could have been one of you—your mother and I would try to live, but we would never be ourselves again," Tim said. "Dave and Bonnie will never be the same." Tim dropped to a crouch by the sofa. "I know it's worse for you than the others because you, Meredith, were there by accident and Mallory, well, you knew. That doesn't excuse you from ordinary human sympathy, girls. Get up now."

Meredith walked as if against a strong current across the cool, blue, peaceful room where canned organ music made her feel as though she were inside a huge cheesy music box. Mallory walked beside her. They felt the stares—just because of the way they looked, so small and so utterly the same.

Everyone knew that Meredith had found David after his fall.

Everyone knew that Mallory had a seizure of some kind the same day.

They were "the twins who saved the kids from the fire," not just "the twins." They were "the twins who were there when Bonnie Jellico's boy fell off the cliff," not just "the twins." Or so they thought.

In fact, no one who saw Mally and Merry felt anything but pity. Nothing had gone right for these little girls this year. They had been through so much, the poor things—from the fire to losing their lifelong friend. Many mothers watched Mallory and Meredith pass and hoped that this could be the end of their innocent suffering. Their hearts embraced the Jellicos, but recognized how much loss the Brynns had endured as well, in six short months. Two families and so close. It must end now, people said to themselves. At least now, perhaps Campbell and Tim's girls could get on with their growing. And in time, poor little Kim.

But as she felt everyone's eyes inch their way over her and her sister, Merry didn't know that. If it had been possible, she would have snapped her fingers and moved their house to Massachusetts or Denver by time travel. She would never see her teammates again, or let them hoist her into her beautifully balanced "lib," or catch her in the basket. She would give it all up. Just to disappear.

Mally didn't notice anyone noticing her twin and her. If only this moment could end, this moment and the funeral tomorrow, she thought. She had never wanted anything more, except for her family to survive—not an iPod, not an honor-roll grade, not to win. With the pessimism and weariness of a disillusioned adult, all she wanted was for this to end.

Finally, both of them stood inches from Kim's bowed head, with its wavy corkscrew curls in messy curtains across her face, and the jacket—that jacket—clutched beneath her chin. Merry thought, *I'll run*. She would turn and run out of the door and run along School Street all the way back to Ridgeline, up onto her porch, up onto the swing, to lie on the swing until her father came home, even if it was morning. All the way back to a childhood when she stepped out onto her porch each summer morning to greetings and approval from everyone on the street, greetings from people who all knew her name and her parents and their parents, smiles and nods that felt to her like the touch of gentle hands. And that had been just a year ago.

But just as Meredith began to turn away, Mallory saved her. It was *Mallory* who knelt down next to Kim.

It would work, Merry thought: The twins were dressed exactly the same. She almost didn't believe it. Mallory was pretending to be her. She sounded just like her. Mallory had removed her earring. Weak with gratitude, Merry reached up and removed hers.

"Kimmy," Mally-as-Merry said. "Kimmy, nothing in the world I can say to you can change this. But you know I love you so, so, so much. And you know I totally cared about David. I would have done anything. I would still do anything. I'm so sorry I was such a silly little girl," Mallory said, in perfect imitation of her sister. "I'll always feel like I was such a stupid idiot. Maybe someday you can forgive me."

"And me," Merry said, mimicking Mallory's diffident, slightly reluctant speech. "That goes for me too, Kim. Honest."

For only the second time since they played baby tricks, Mallory went on pretending to be her sister. She stood the way Merry stood. She smiled the way Merry smiled. *Thank you, Ster,* Merry thought.

Kim didn't move or look up, and the group of girls around them seemed collectively to hold their breath. Merry thought, *I'll scream and scream and scream and scream. . . .*

And then Kim got up and threw her arms around Mallory-as-Merry and gasped, "I thought you didn't care at all!"

Mallory-as-Merry began to cry—that wasn't hard—and said, "How could you think that? I was just staying away because I felt like such an idiot. . . ."

"You don't think he killed himself, do you, Mer? You don't think that. The police thought maybe because of how hard it would have been to climb up there that he killed himself. But why would David kill himself? He had everything he wanted. Girls and grades and looks! We all loved him so much. My big brother. My only big brother."

The real Merry began to cry as well.

That was true enough. Despite everything, Kim had lost the only brother she would ever have, unless Bonnie and David adopted a Chinese baby or something. And they were old, at least probably forty, like her parents.

Still holding Kim close, Mallory-as-Merry said, "I know he didn't kill himself, Kim. I know. He was just getting rocks for all those poor cats and dogs. I'm sure he climbed up and down the ridge all the time. It was probably just slippery because there was always a little ice up there this time of year. I'm sure David loves you so much, still, Kimmy. I'm sure he knows how bad you're hurting."

"Did you see if he moved? Do you think he was in pain?" Kim asked.

"Oh, no. I'm sure he never even knew," the pretend Merry said.

Please, no, please, the real Meredith thought, remembering David's scream.

"They were going to dig up his pet place," said Kim.

"Oh, they won't do that to Bonnie," Merry said, pretending to be Mally, using Mally's firm manner of speech. "You just explain how he had such a soft spot for animals. Some people are like that. David didn't do anything wrong." *What else is buried there?* Merry thought. *What else?*

It was almost over, thought Mallory. It was almost over. And it would all be over. And someday no one but Kim's family would remember. They would grow up, and go to college—in California. No one would know them as the fire-and-death-fall girls. They would just be twins.

Just plain twins.

"Will you still be my friend?" Kim asked.

"Of course I will," Mallory said, on her sister's behalf. "Why wouldn't I be?"

The real Merry thought, *I should be. How can I be?*

Kim's father passed by, gently patting each of the twins' backs. He stopped and laid his hands on the place where David's head would be, inside the casket.

Meredith thought she would throw up for sure then. Behind

her, she could hear Bonnie—crying, she supposed, but not like any crying Merry had ever heard, more like the sound of someone being cut open while she was awake, trying to act like it didn't hurt. Tim came and told them they needed to go home, that Campbell would need their help tomorrow and so would Bonnie. The girls grabbed their Ridgeline letter jackets, sprinting for the car. But they didn't escape before they heard Deirdre Bradshaw's comment—a meow and not a whisper. "*There* they are, Grumpy and Dopey. Wonder how they feel now?"

But in the same instant, they heard someone else say, "Shut your face. Those little girls have more going for them now than you ever will." Mallory recognized Eden's voice.

And Trevor Solwyn added, "Mally and Merry are our friends. People here love them. That's how it is." The twins turned as one to stare in amazement at notoriously snippy Trevor. "Well," she said. "It's true! *Me* putting you down is one thing. I'm not going to stand for her doing it!"

THE TWO-HEARTED GIFT

THE TWO-HEARTED GIFT

Everyone else at the Brynn family camp was taking advantage of the soft late July afternoon, scrambling into bathing suits from the previous year and complaining that either they were fatter or the suits had shrunk. A swim before dinner was a family tradition. The dip left everyone relaxed, refreshed, and hungry, ready for a meal, a fire, and the kind of night's sleep they got nowhere else on earth. All of Arthur and Gwenny's children were there. Tim, Kevin, and Karin brought their families, and the youngest, Aunt Jenny from Portland, brought the man she would marry in the fall. Even Grandpa Arthur's father, Walker, was there, annoyed at being called "spry" at nearly ninety.

"It's just another word for saying I'm still able to move without batteries," he told Tim. Jenny and her fiancé, Aaron, were staying with Walker in the big cabin—for safekeeping.

Even this annoyed him.

The girls overheard Tim telling Campbell he just couldn't

imagine a summer, someday, at the camp without his grandfather.

"He can't last forever, but there are some parts of your life you just wish could," Tim said softly. "This day is one."

"And I can think of a few that you don't," Campbell replied. The twins knew what she meant. They were grateful to have emerged from the grief and fear of the past six months with their sanity and their reputations intact. It could really have gone another way. Instead, Ridgeline seemed to have closed around the twins and David's family with love, support, and the gentleness to avoid too many questions.

Mally and Merry were about to grab their own suits when Grandma Gwenny stopped them.

"I'd like to have green beans from the garden to go alongside the corn tonight," Gwenny said. "But I don't think I can snap all of them by myself. Would you girls help me?"

It wasn't really a question. Both of them knew what was coming and that it wouldn't be a discussion of green beans. But in a sense, they welcomed it. What would Grandma say, Mallory wondered? Merry suspected that Grandma might want a debriefing on what really happened with David Jellico. Both were curious about what she might say. She seemed to say so much without ever saying hardly anything at all.

For just a moment, as her family departed, Merry resented not being able to go with them. The day was damp and hot, and the water would be glorious. Then she remembered the riverbank. The swimming hole was far down and around a bend from the place where David landed when he fell. Still, Merry figured it would take her most of the two weeks that her family was staying to work her way down into the river—even though she'd swum in this water since she was a baby.

So she sat down on the lowest step, beside Mallory. Grandma gave each girl a huge bowl and a brown paper bag for the popped ends, which they would burn in the fire pit. They spread a light blanket over their laps and set to work. Hannah, Alex, and Adam— always the last ones—went pounding past with their towels. They seemed to have grown six inches since winter—to Mally and Meredith's measly half inch. They sometimes thought that this fraction of height would be the last one they would ever get.

They were right.

Grandma asked about cheerleading tryouts, and seemed gently amazed that Meredith had actually made junior varsity, though she would be on probationary status to see if she could keep up her performance and grades through football season. Mally would try out for the high school soccer team in just two weeks.

For a while, the only sound was the plink of the plucked beans falling into the big canning pot.

The lull seemed to stretch out like commercials during the Super Bowl. It finally made Merry so jumpy that she blurted out the fact that, after David's death, the dreams had stopped. Drew Vaughan, she added, was the only other person on earth who knew this. She joked: Drew was grateful—on his own behalf. As he told Mallory, if next year was anything like last, he'd never have gas money again.

"It's great to just be here and feel like ourselves again," Merry said. Her answer was only silence. They still couldn't see each other's dreams, she went on, but they had come to accept this.

Safe at camp, surrounded only by people who loved them . . . they no longer felt the burden of adult fears and forebodings. Mally wore unfashionably patched and worn cutoffs with one of Drew's wretched old shirts, and Merry a bikini top over jean shorts she had artfully and carefully destroyed with bleach and scissors.

They were contented almost to the point of dozing off when Grandma Gwenny said, "You're so happy. Not like all year, like little frightened deer. My sweet ones, I hate to say a thing."

The mellow sun seemed to wink out. Merry felt the goose bumps rise on her arms.

It was Mallory who asked, slowly, "What do you mean, Grandma?"

"I know you think that it's all over," Gwenny answered, even more gently. "That it will never come back."

"It is," Mally said. "He was evil. But he's not a vampire, Grandma. He's not coming back."

"I don't mean that boy. I mean the sight," said Grandma, and the twins stopped snapping the little peaked caps off the beans.

"What about it?" Merry asked. "That was a one-time-only thing. Wasn't it? Because we were supposed to save the kids? And whoever David was going to hurt?"

Slowly, Gwenny shook her head. "You have to know about your history, now that you know about your future."

"Our future?" Mallory cried. "Grandma, it's not going to happen again, the dream and the whole big dance that goes with it? Is it? Grandma?"

Gwenny sighed. "Let me try to make you see the chain."

She cupped her chin in her hands and glanced up into the trees.

"I'll bet you thought we were alone—just the two of you and me, who were like this," she said. The girls nodded. "But that's not true. Twins don't run through the Brynns, but through my side. The Massengers. My mother was an identical twin, and so was her mother, and so was I. And all of us had the sight."

The girls were too stunned to speak.

Their grandmother went on, "If I had to say, I'd guess that it wasn't as strong for any of us as it is for you." Mallory nodded, unsure of what she was approving. "Alice, my grandmother, and her sister—that was Aunt Annie—they saw our female ancestors. Just saw the past as it was lived. Like you see the past, Merry. Annie saw the recent past, the ones who had passed over, saying good-bye. Alice saw the long past. All the Massengers who came from Wales, oh, ten, twelve generations ago. The men were miners and some farmers. This camp was actually built near some ground that my family owned. They hoped it would be a mine, for zinc or salt. An old uncle bought it with his last bit of savings."

Gwenny got up to open another bag of beans. Mallory thought that if her grandmother didn't speed things up, she would jump out of her scalp. Why did old people insist on dragging every story out for hours? Maybe it was because they were used to people not paying much attention to them—but that wasn't the case with Grandma Gwenny. She was always on the go, messing around in her four hundred or so flower beds, going hiking with her friends. ("My mother-in-law has better thighs than I do," Campbell complained.) She even brought food to "the elderly," as if she, Gwenny, were still "the youngerly."

But since no one ever got her to do anything any other way but her own, Mallory took some deep breaths until her grandmother resumed the story. "All this land is Brynn land. And what isn't is Massenger land. Our families grew up nearly side by side, Arthur's and mine. We knew each other from when we were Adam's age. In fact, my grandmother's ashes were buried near that place where that Jellico boy died. She died young, of influenza, during the epidemic."

Meredith's skin crawled with the telltale chill. *If the woman died young . . .*

"Did your grandmother have this thick white hair? Beautiful hair? So she looked old but was really sort of young? As in, young like my mother, but white-haired?" Meredith asked.

"She did have hair just like that," Gwenny said. "Have you seen her, Merry?"

"Yes," Meredith said, as though they were talking about the best thing to use on a sunburn.

"Up there?"

"Yes," Merry said. "And in dreams."

"I have, too," Gwenny said. "It's a comfort. I loved her so. And did you see my sister?"

"I don't know. I don't know how your sister looked."

"Why, she looked like any little girl, I suppose," Grandma Gwenny said. "Of course, we wore skirts then, not trousers so much. She had black hair, just like you, and wore it long in a braid. So did I."

Merry thought of her hospital visions, of the little girl on the bridge with the great sad eyes, rushing toward her.

"I guess I have, Grandma. I saw her standing on a bridge over a river or a creek."

Gwenny said sadly, "I guess you would have seen her there. Did she see you?"

"She looked at me," Merry admitted, with a gulp.

"Me too," Mallory said. "We thought she was a hallucination."

"No, not that. Not at all. I'm sure she actually looked at you."

"That's just great," Mallory told her, covering her eyes. "Hello! The sister from another generation."

"I'm sure she loves you very much and wishes she could meet you in this world, girls. She was the sweet one, my twin sister. I was the toughie."

"Grandma, what did you and your sister see?" Mallory asked.

"Well, let's talk about my mother, Catherine, and her sister, Corinna, first."

"Okay," Mally agreed.

"Now, my mother, Cathy, could look into anyone's past or present and see more than life the way it was lived, more than my grandmother saw. She could see into the secrets. Anyone in any town. She could see sad things, like illnesses. She could see love people felt and fear and anger. It was just like the houses didn't have walls. You can imagine, she had to keep so much to herself, though of course, she could tell Aunt Nini! There were quite a few babies born who weren't the sons of the fathers whose names they had! Quite a few women who wore white wedding gowns . . . but this isn't really talk for you kids."

"What about Corinna?" Mallory asked.

"Corinna. We called her Aunt Nini," Gwenny said. "She could see inside people, not houses. She could see what they were really thinking, no matter what awful thing was behind a big smile."

"Now that would be the kind I'd like to have!" Meredith said. "I'd love to know who was talking about me. I'd love to know if someone was getting—"

"Laybite, Merry. For heaven's sake," Mallory said. She turned to her grandmother and persisted, "But you. And your sister."

"Well, you know, I have never told you about my sister."

"But we know she died when she was little," Merry said.

"Not little. Only in size. Like you are. She was eleven. She drowned, my dears. And ever after, I never felt quite the same. Not even with Grandpa and the children, as dearly as I love all of you. I still grieve for her, sixty years later and more." Gwenny sighed and said, "But she was . . . I would say that she was born sad. Vera."

"Why?" asked Mallory, certain that she knew.

"I think because we . . . well, we were the first ones in the family to foresee the future. I saw the births, the weddings, the letters in the mailboxes that brought hope from far away, the happy beginnings. But Vera saw the endings. She foresaw death."

Mallory let her hands drop into her lap. Broken beans scattered in the dirt.

"Vera saw the babies who would be born with something wrong, even while they were still inside their mothers and the girls were knitting little blankets and thanking God for answering their prayers. She told me, but, of course, she could never tell anyone else. She would have been seen to be crazy, or even worse—cursed or witched or something. What she saw couldn't be changed, you understand. It wasn't as though she'd been asked to intervene. And she knew it."

Merry was about to interrupt when Gwenny said, "Let's get these beans finished. We're going to have to have supper and I want your brother to shuck the corn. I really should set the water boiling for that, too."

"But Grandma, go on," Meredith prompted her.

"I know I'm rambling, Merry. I don't like to say it. It's been years since I talked about my Vera. I think she was tormented because she didn't have the gift you have, to step in front of fate. She foresaw our father's death in the mines. She foresaw it, and begged him not to go that day. Of course, he didn't listen. We were nine. Moira was fourteen and Jane was twelve. Thea was sixteen, already working in the city. The little boys, our brothers, were four and two. After the accident, Vera never told our mother. How could she have lived with knowing her own little girl might have saved her daddy? We moved to just this side of Deptford, at first, to a boardinghouse near the wider part of this river. My mother cleaned houses and took in fine sewing. She left the care of the little boys to us when she went out to work. The only schooling we had after that was what she taught us at home. But she tried hard to teach us well. She saved her money and bought us schoolbooks that the library was selling for a nickel or a dime."

"You were too young," said Merry.

"Not for those times," Gwenny told her. Laughter and splashing sang up the path from the swimmers below. Grandma seemed to tense at the sound. "Yes, you should know that it's water that is dangerous for us, for all of us, we Massenger women. That was why I knew the fire wouldn't truly hurt you."

"You . . . knew about the fire?" Mallory breathed softly.

"I didn't really. Not as such. What I felt was that Vera knew about the fire. I felt something, from her. Not a message of death. But a message. At least, I seemed to. Sometimes, I think I hear her speak to me. But you see, I can't get in the way of changing fate. Not as you can. There was nothing I could do. I didn't know when it would happen or how."

"Did . . . did our aunt Vera know she was going to die?"

"You never know about yourself," Grandma Gwenny said.

"Why didn't I see David coming for Merry?" asked Mallory. "Because she is just like myself? I saw at the last minute, when it was too late."

"I don't know why," Grandma Gwenny said. "I don't know everything." Her eyes filled. "Just to tell you the last thing. Vera lost her footing."

"She was on that bridge. . . ." Mallory said.

"Yes, and she saw our younger brother, your uncle Keenan, who was too little to know better, wade in after a shiny rock, and saw him slip. That is, before he slipped. She ran to help."

"Did you see her drown?" Merry asked.

"No. But I saw her afterward," Gwenny said. A hunger and an anger crossed her face as quickly as clouds and did not invite more questions. "I hoped she was happy then."

"Why didn't your names match?" Meredith asked, as much from curiosity as to distract her grandmother from the memory picture she could almost see—of her grandmother's still, small sister, lying on a kitchen table with water pooling around her blue

cotton dress, strands of water lily in her dark hair. "Not that they
have to match. But people do that when they have twins."

"Well, our names did match. Her name was Guinevere. We
called her Vera. Now, I suppose it would be Jenny; that's what we
call your aunt. I named my youngest for her. In Welsh, it means
'the shadow in front of the light.' And my name, Gwendolyn,
means 'white hair.' I thought of that when my hair went white so
young, like my grandma's did."

"Why aren't your daughters twins?" Mallory asked.

"Well, Karin was a twin," Gwenny said slowly. "But her sister
died before she was born. No one knew except for me. Not even
Grandpa."

"So you saw us?" Merry asked.

"Not only that. I know when a baby will be healthy. Not . . .
as much as I did when Vera was here. Well, alive on earth. But I
knew you two would be the ones who would see both the past and
the future. The greatest gift."

"And you were *jealous* of that?" Mallory asked, aghast.

"Oh, my goodness no! I was proud. But I felt such pity, too!
My poor little granddaughters. The gift has two sides, Merry. The
brilliant side and the misery. And I know that it must have been
as hard on you as on Mallory. You would always know what had
happened if you and Mallory didn't act on what she saw coming
up ahead. You would never be free to simply not know. Such an
amazing gift."

"No, a curse!" Meredith said. "But, Grandma, the dreams
stopped. It all started just before the fire, and ended when we
stopped . . . when David Jellico died," Merry went on. "We don't

dream of the past and the future anymore. We dream of boys and . . . like, showing up for school in your underwear. Regular stuff."

"But this is what I kept you back from swimming to tell you," their grandmother said. "You will."

"No," Mallory said.

Gwenny nodded. After a long moment simply looking from one to the other, she said, "You'll always know. Not every day or even every month. Not ever for yourselves, though perhaps for each other. But always for other people in need or trouble."

"We don't want it!" Mally said.

Gwenny put her arm around Mallory. She said, "You poor babies. None of us ever did. It's given. I had to tell you. Even knowing what's going on inside a house could be a torment. You might know that the mayor beat his children. You might know a widow's son was packing to run off and join the army. Or who was lonely and wanted to die. It sounds like that might be fun, but Mama said it wasn't."

"But if you had to have one kind, I'd rather have that one," Merry insisted. "It wouldn't be scary and boring at the same time!"

Grandma seemed to ignore Merry in her haste to get the story told. The sun was setting. Soon, everyone would come back and dinner and campfire rituals would take over and the girls would have to wait. That would have been fine with Merry, who believed she had heard enough to last a lifetime. Mallory would break out in hives if she had to live another day without hearing the rest.

"You were the first ones born to one of the boys, not to a Messenger woman, the first twins born to a son," Grandma said.

"Big deal," Merry told her with a shrug.

"She doesn't mean that to be rude. We just wonder why it matters. Because this is the worst thing that ever happened to us," Mallory added. "To think of it happening once more is too horrible to imagine. To think of it happening over and over, it would be better if we'd never been born."

"Mallory, I'm sure even our Lord felt that way, when he knew what his work was in the world. Think of the good you've already done! You've saved the children, already more good than most people do in their whole lives. In that sense, it truly is a gift."

"We would have saved them anyhow, even if Mally hadn't dreamed of a fire. It's really, really not a gift at all, Grandma," Merry said.

"Maybe not to you. I can't pretend to say why this is given. Maybe to the world."

"Well, the kids are safe now. And the way I feel is, the world can go to hell!" Merry objected.

"Hush! Merry," their grandmother said. "Every time it happens, you'll be confused, or even frightened, but then you'll know you have to try to help. And you'll know how, I think."

"I don't want to know," Mally said. "I want to be happy!"

"You'll be happy," Gwenny said.

"Not if we know this is coming," said Mallory. "Not if I know there's something I'm going to see happen and she's going to see it really did. That's why I'm going to be a nun!"

"You're not going to be a nun, Mallory," said Grandma Gwenny. "And you couldn't hide from this if you were. Think about it. Yes, it's awful to think of it coming. But what if you can change things so that the bad doesn't happen? Isn't that like changing the world?"

"What if we can't? What if we don't know how?" Mallory asked.

"I don't know," said their grandmother. "You're unique. I don't know if you'll always be able to make it right."

"But even if we do, no one will ever know," Merry said. "Even if we do good, if we told anyone about it, people would think we were nuts."

"*You* will know," said their grandmother.

"Why couldn't we be like you? And just be able to predict the next baby who'll be born down the street?" Merry asked.

"If I had to, I'd guess that because you're the daughters of so many generations of wisdom that it isn't enough for you to see, but for you to be able to save. To be like Saint Bridget, the brave, and comfort the helpless and protect the weak," said Gwenny. "It must seem impossible. But here you are. So strong and bright."

"I don't want to be a saint! Only a nun! And then only because I could hide and not have to worry about clothes. How do you know this isn't from some old time when things were dark and wicked? How do you know it's a thing that comes from God and not demons?" Mallory asked. She was conscious of the hills around her, the dark mosses and teasing shadows, the chill of twilight and of the birds gone silent. "Who'll protect us and comfort us?"

"You'll comfort each other. No matter how many miles there are between you, you'll never be farther apart than you are right now. And that will make the gift something you'll share, and even learn to cherish. Not everything ancient is wicked, Mally-lah."

"How do you know, Grandma?" Mally asked, as something in her sighed deeply and turned up its hands. There was no fighting it, she thought. *This is not why I dreamed that the fire would happen. This is the reason that we were born.*

"It was what I saw," Gwenny said. "What I saw on your parents' wedding day. I saw you girls and Adam. And I thought . . . there would be another child. But I was wrong about that, I suppose."

"You mean it's not even always perfect? You don't always see everything exactly as it is?" Mallory asked, aghast.

"Nothing is perfect," Grandma said.

Meredith watched as first Campbell and Tim, then their aunts and uncles and cousins, and finally their brother straggled up the path, toweling off their hair and brushing at their sandy legs. It was with a certain sadness, as though she would never see them again in quite this way—which was, of course, true.

"All I wanted was to make junior varsity," Merry said.

Fresh, lined paper and cucumber lotion and the smell of a boy's newly cut hair, her father's omelets, huge as sea creatures and dripping with butter and four kinds of cheese, a bowl of pinecones dipped in glitter on the kitchen table and the shrieking of the crowd under the lights and a Twizzler fossilized in the pocket of her winter coat—all these little simple things that made up her life before seemed to whirl together and blow out like a spent star.

"Grandma," Mallory asked, "will you help us? If we don't know where to turn? That was the worst part. We didn't even know how much we could tell you. What if we don't know what to do?"

"As long as I live. And I don't plan on going anywhere soon. I'll listen, but I might not know what to do," Gwenny said. "I'm not so powerful as you are. And after I'm gone, I'll listen, as well."

"Don't say that, Grandma!" Merry cried, and Mallory shook her head, too. It was enough to take all this in. It was too much to picture a world without Grandma Gwenny.

"So we won't be alone," Mallory said.

"Not ever," said their grandmother. "The Massenger women, your ancestors, are always with you. They always will be. They're all around you. They will guide you. You're not invincible. But you have protection. And so will your daughters . . ."

"It stops here," Merry said. "There won't be any more twins."

Their grandmother pressed her lips together before she told them gently, "No, that's not true. Mallory will have twin daughters. And you, Merry, will have three sons."

Merry looked down at the scar on her hand. It had healed to resemble a tree. The longest branch extended to the edge of her palm. One branch split into two, which in turn split into two. She nudged Mallory. For a long moment, she studied the scar and its portents.

"Ster," she finally said to Mallory. "You're the one who never wanted to be typical."

"I got over it," Mally murmured, studying the toes of her running shoes.

"But if you are, you are. I mean, it's going to be harder for me. I'm a cheerleader!"

"Oh, yeah," Mally said scornfully. "I can see that! It's easy to be a freak if you aren't a fruitcake with plastic pom-poms, too!"

"Mallory, I'm only saying. If we can't fight it, we have no other choice but to join it. We have to find a way that it doesn't control us. We have to learn the way it works and use it to make it work. That's what you *do*, Mallory. Maybe it could . . . could almost be interesting."

"Like a rare skin disease could be interesting," Mallory replied. Then she breathed deeply and raised her head. "Only thing is, I guess if you have to be a freak, at least it's better to be a freak who can do something to help . . . somehow."

"Especially if you have no choice."

"There's that," Mallory agreed, her eyes glum.

"Let's take a run," Merry suggested. "Before dinner. We never ran up this far, or past the camp. Let's go farther up the road."

"You go," Mally said. "That road goes straight up. I just want to be a vegetable. I have to sleep this off."

"You'll sleep your life away," Merry teased her. "You going off to nap is just the same as me trying to put it out of my mind."

"Maybe it is," Mally agreed. "Maybe I was wrong. Let's both put it out of our minds. Anyhow, I can't sleep. What if I have a *dream*? Okay. I'll go if we run all the way to Canada, not just to the end of Canada Road."

Merry shrugged. Then, handing over her bowl of snapped beans to her grandmother, she stretched her calves and set off.

Within ten minutes, she was so far up the steep path she could feel it in her lungs. She rounded a bend and, through the scrubby trees, caught sight of the camp—a ring of old cabins and a bare patch of ground so far below and behind her that she hardly recognized it. Up here, where few people except a few hikers and backpackers used it, the path narrowed and veered closer to the jagged brow of cliff on her right. If she stopped and leaned over the side, she would see down, down, down—to the rocks on the riverbed. While the sky above was still bright, shadows seeped into the spaces at the bases of trees, making the way ahead dim. Then, behind her, she heard the unmistakable slurry rasp of pebbles sliding away under the feet of someone faster, coming up behind. Merry stumbled. Her throat refused to open. She thought of that morning, alone on the path, of David's guttural voice, his face distorted by rage. Merry stumbled. She cried out with her mind, *Mally!*

The footsteps stopped.

A single pebble rolled.

Then she heard Mally thinking to her: *It's me.*

Just where the path widened, Mally was waiting. She laughed. "Beester!" she said, panting, bending to grasp her knees. "This is straight up! I couldn't catch you!"

"I'm fast now. I'm not a big sissy anymore."

"Sure you are," Mallory teased. "I heard you up there. You were about to start bawling!"

Merry pushed past her twin. Mallory reached out, but Merry jerked away. Turning to face Mally, she said, "You know, Mallory? You're so tough. But you weren't here. You didn't hear the disgusting things he said. You never saw anybody die. You never saw the white thing that came . . ."

"No. You're right," said Mally. "I was never here. But I felt what you felt. I thought I would die, too. Are you glad he fell?"

For a long moment, Merry didn't answer. Mallory couldn't see her face. "I'm glad it's over," she said finally. "At least, that part is over."

She took Mallory's hand. "Everything is okay now. Or at least, it's as okay as it can be. I know you hate it, but we can't change the future. Well, I mean, we *can* change the future, but we can't change this power . . . or whatever it is. All we can do is live with it. And the only thing harder than dealing with it would be dealing with it alone." Meredith stopped. When she continued, it was in a voice more serious than Mally had ever heard her use. "I've been thinking, Mal. Maybe that's all you get. The only bonus is someone to help you bear it. I don't think anything can drive you crazy if you have somebody to share it with. At least, that's my idea and I'm sticking to it."

For the first time since they were in kindergarten, and frightened by the boys on the big slide, Mallory squeezed Merry's hand instead of pulling away. After a moment, Merry released her. They began to walk, tentatively, in the dusk. For a moment, the only sound was the crunch of their steps.

Then Merry said, "Look. Just down there. You can see the campfire. All we have to do is stay together and stick to the path. I'll go first. I'm getting used to seeing in the dark."

Acknowledgments

This is a work of fiction, but twin telepathy is very real (although not to the degree here posited). For their assistance in helping me understand it, I thank "the grown-up twins," who knew (telepathically, I am sure) how to find me at book signings and events all over the country, as well as L.C., who allowed me to observe her five-year-old daughters at play. Plotting this book needed all I could give, never having written a mystery. For this, I am grateful to friends and colleagues Sara Pennypacker, Anne D. LeClaire, Jodi Picoult, Holly Kennedy, Andy Scontras, Jana K. Felt, Susan Schofield, Michael Schofield, John Fetto, Lisa Alexander, and Dr. Ann Collins, all of whom gave me essential suggestions in helping create Meredith and Mallory's world. Ben Schrank of Razorbill has the lightest hands on the bit of any editor I have ever met, and I am thrilled that he and I will work together on two more Midnight Twins novels. For plot advice, I thank my son, Daniel Brent-Allegretti. To my cousins, Rayna Cardinal Shawa and Bridget Cardinal Swallow, for their love and insight into our common Canadian/American Indian heritage, I send best love. Enduring gratitude goes to the Ragdale Foundation, where this book was written in 2007. My agent, Jane (Sadie) Gelfman, has my heart, always, as do my cherished friends, my estimable husband, and my seven astounding children.